Gaelle Lehrer Kennedy

NIGHT IN JERUSALEM

a novel

Gaelle Lehrer Kennedy

PKZ Publishing
12121 Wilshire Boulevard, Suite 800
Los Angeles, California 90025 USA

Dust-jacket and interior design by Russell Martin
and Say Yes Quickly Books. www.sayyesquickly.net
Ordering Information:

Discounts are available on quantity purchases by corporations, associations, and others. For details, contact the Special Sales Department at the address above.

Night in Jerusalem / Gaelle Lehrer Kennedy. -- 1st ed.
ISBN 978-0-9965592-1-8

If I forget thee, O Jerusalem,
let my right hand forget her cunning.

—PSALM 137

For my mother, Yitkah Lehrer

NIGHT IN JERUSALEM

ONE

Hail pounded the windshield of the *sherut* as it made its way through the night to Jerusalem. The driver pulled to the side of the road, startled. He peered at the windshield. It was fractured, but to his astonishment, still intact.

"In twenty years I never see such storm," he said in his best English.

He lit a cigarette and offered the pack to his passengers. David refused; the three Israelis accepted. Sitting up front, an elderly woman took out oranges, which she peeled, divided, and shared, using her dress to wipe the juice off her hands. The taxi filled with the pungent smell of oranges mixed with cigarette smoke. David cracked open a window.

The storm reminded him of the monsoon in India. Like many of his generation, he had gone there searching for revelation. He had hoped it would let him shake off the feeling of isolation that plagued him wherever he went. His upbringing had given him every comfort that money could buy, except the comfort of belonging in his own skin. At times the loneliness hid long enough to fool him into thinking it was gone, but then, like a familiar ghost, it would find its way back and fill him with despair. After a year of traveling, he had returned to England, only to discover that nothing had changed.

Now, stuck in a taxi on a desolate hilltop outside Jerusalem, enveloped by smoke while waiting out the storm, he regretted leaving Hampshire's gentle slopes, which were always so green and welcoming, where sometimes after a rain, like a gift from heaven, the sun would come out followed by a sudden rainbow.

He was trying to ignore his reservations about coming to Israel. He wished he had not allowed his cousin to persuade him to come "just for a visit." Although Jonathan, at twenty-eight, was only a year older, David viewed him as a more mature, elder brother, as well as his best friend. They had grown up together in the south of England in an aristocratic family, enjoying the privileges of great wealth, but subject to the remoteness from society that it can sometimes bring. When Jonathan had left for Israel, David's loneliness had become unbearable.

After an hour, the storm stopped. The driver told everyone they would need another car to take them to Jerusalem, as he could not see out of his cracked windshield, and that their only option, given the hour, was to hitchhike. The passengers stood at the side of the road for what seemed like an eternity. David was certain he would be there until morning, when an army truck loomed out of the night and juddered to a stop. The driver, a young soldier, helped them aboard, before continuing cautiously down the steep, winding road to Jerusalem.

David was the last passenger to be dropped off. He thanked the soldier for stopping and delivering them safely, surprised by the informality of it all. Just after midnight, standing before a two-story stone building in Abu Tor, with only the moon shimmering through the clouds for illumination, he could just about make out the number of the house. The flat Jonathan had arranged for him was upstairs. He could not find the light and, after blindly climbing the staircase, he felt his way to the top-floor door and fumbled under the mat for the key.

Inside the flat, a lamp had been left on for him, with a note attached to a bottle of wine on a small, wooden table.

Welcome to Jerusalem. See you in the morning, eight o'clock at Cafe Cassis. It's down the hill to Hebron Road, then right to Rehov (Street) King David, and right again on Rehov Ben-Yehudah. The cafe will be on your right, just a bit further up at the corner. It's less than a fifteen-minute walk, Jonathan.

P.S. If you want a bath, turn on the red switch outside the loo an hour before. Hope you remembered to bring toilet paper.

The shutters on the windows and doors were closed. The room had a vaulted ceiling and contained a dark, birch armoire that matched the headboard on the double bed. A tufted, deep green armchair was the only other piece of furniture. The room felt as ancient as the city.

Chilled from the storm, David lit the gas heater, then clicked on the red switch for hot water. The bathroom had a commode with a chain flush and a small sink with an even smaller mirror above it. He felt the rough, brown toilet paper sitting on top of the commode and understood why Jonathan had told him to bring a suitcase full. He was grateful there was a deep bathtub with a hand shower.

Restless while waiting for the water to heat, he changed into warmer clothes and decided to take a first look at the city he would live in for the next month.

Outside, the narrow, winding roads of Abu Tor had been soaked by the storm. The stone houses were dark and there were no streetlights. The place seemed uninhabited, with only feral cats out searching for food. Wandering the neighborhood deepened his sense of isolation. He knew nothing of Israel, did not speak the language and, besides Jonathan, knew no one in the country. How could a month here relieve his despair?

Had Jonathan been there to meet him at the flat, he would have felt better, but Jonathan lived near the University of Jerusalem, where he was studying Judaism. Tonight he had gone to a seminar in Haifa and would not be returning until the morning.

David climbed up a steep road, unable to see anything but the stone wall beside him when, suddenly, at the top of the hill, Jerusalem's Old City revealed itself. The lights peering from stone houses built neatly into its hills shimmered with golden hues against the night. It was, as Jonathan had promised, mysterious and beautiful.

Soaking in a hot bath gave him a restful night until he was awakened at six by a loudspeaker calling the Muslims to prayer, "*Allah, Akbar...*" Sleepily, he opened the shutters and doors which led onto the roof and there, again, was a panoramic view of Jerusalem. He felt the warmth of the sun as it rose from behind Mount Zion, with no sign of last night's storm. The clear, blue sky amplified the city's magnificence. He could see a crescent of cypress trees and, below it, the walled Old City with its minarets and church spires. He looked out at the Church of the Holy Sepulcher and the golden dome of Al-Aqsa Mosque glittering in the sun. To the far left stood the King David Hotel. He felt a surprising surge of excitement.

He had an hour before meeting Jonathan at Café Cassis and, eager to get a feeling for the city, decided to take a leisurely stroll to the café. By seven o'clock, most of the businesses were open. He passed the King David Hotel and a small cafe where the smell of coffee and freshly-baked pita bread filled the street, already bustling with people, rickety buses, Volkswagens and Mini Minors.

Arriving at the café, he immediately spotted a bearded Jonathan sitting reading the *Jerusalem Post.* Jonathan jumped up and hugged him.

"Great to see you! I've been so looking forward to you being here. I can't believe you've finally shown up. How's the flat?"

"Fine, the views are spectacular."

"Well it's yours for two years, if you like. The chap who owns it is on sabbatical in Argentina. He'd be delighted to get the rent."

"I've committed for a month," David reminded him, so as to not get Jonathan's hopes up. "You look very Jewie with that beard. Do you have to have one to study Judaism?"

"Very funny."

"How are the studies going?"

"Really well, actually. How was your trip to India?"

"A bit challenging. After one of their downpours, my car got stuck in the mud and started sinking. I thought I was going to be swallowed up. I took it as my cue to leave." David looked at the thick, muddy coffee Jonathan was drinking, "I hope they've got more than that to drink."

"How about a cup of tea?"

"Perfect. Do they serve eggs with sausages?"

"Yes, more or less."

Jonathan introduced David to Uri, the owner of the café, then, in Hebrew, ordered their breakfast.

"It's good to see you, Jonathan. I've missed you," David confessed.

"By the way, I've arranged for you to meet with the rebbe tomorrow."

"I know how you feel about him, but frankly, I'm not much interested in meeting him," David said, as gently as he could, not wanting Jonathan to feel his good intentions were unappreciated.

"David, I'm just asking you to be open-minded. The rebbe has helped so many people. They come from all over the world just to meet him. Why not give him a try? You've got nothing to lose."

"Why are you so keen for me to see him? What's so special about him?"

"That's something you're going to have to find out for yourself, but I promise, once you meet him, you will be hungry for more."

"More of what?"

"You'll see. He's helped me enormously," Jonathan said emphatically.

David sat quietly, absorbing what Jonathan was saying. He felt envious of his enthusiasm and that he had found his place in the world.

"Jonathan, I don't know if this is ..."

Before he could finish, Jonathan interrupted, "Give it a try. There's no harm in looking into your own heritage."

"It's not my heritage. I know absolutely nothing about it. You know how it is at home. All we do is make an appearance at the Synagogue on Yom Kippur, when of course, it's a delight to spend quality time with the other closet Jews."

"Sarcasm has always been such a part of your charm, David."

"Have you forgotten that my mother thought you 'troubled' when you told us you were coming here? And how we were instructed 'the situation' was 'best kept to ourselves.' Heaven forbid it would jeopardize her luncheon invitations from the queen."

Although it was all true, Jonathan reasoned, "David it's what we were born into. Why not give it a chance. Nobody is asking you to commit to anything."

"Good, because I have no intention of becoming more of a Jew, or anything else for that matter. This country is like any other country, as far as I'm concerned. I'm not here on any kind of pilgrimage."

"I'm so glad you haven't changed."

Uri brought David his tea along with their breakfast of scrambled eggs, a few thin slices of salami and a crusty roll. Jonathan caught David eyeing the salami with suspicion. "Think of it as fine-pressed sausage."

Reb Eliezer Ben-Yaacov, known to everyone as "Reb Eli," sat quietly in the study hall of his synagogue in Mea Shearim while his Torah students debated the meaning of *Chanukah*, the Festival of Lights. The previous night's storm had kept him awake, leaving him weary for today's studies. Whenever the rebbe couldn't sleep, he sat and read his favorite verses from the great *Tzaddikim,* those awakened souls who had come to such a tenderness towards the world that they saw only its beauty. But last night, despite his reading, he had been unable to stop worrying about his youngest daughter.

It had been ten years since his wife had died. Still, he felt God had been generous with him. He was blessed with five children. He had all that he needed, and, three years previously, to his surprise, he had been named Chief Rabbi of Jerusalem. Based on his growing reputation as a sage, people came from all over the world to seek his guidance. But he could not resolve his concerns about his own daughter. He lived among the Hasidim, and whenever he walked by, the women would become suddenly silent. He knew what they were saying about Sarah. "Blessed with beauty, cursed with misfortune, a woman born luckless, without *mazel.*"

Sarah was just twelve years old when her mother died. His eldest daughter, Dvorah, had taken on the burden of being her mother. She already had three children of her own. She did her best to look after Sarah as well.

Reb Eli was delighted when Sarah married Yossi, a kind, scholarly young man from a pious family. But after three years of marriage, she was still childless when her devoted husband was stricken with a rare form of cancer and died. All in Mea Shearim gossiped, "Poor, beautiful Sarah had so many bees, but no honey." The sadness in his daughter's eyes weighed heavily on him.

Reb Eli was brought back from his troubled thoughts by Chaim, a slight young man from a family of fourteen children whose curiosity and devoted scholarship made him one of the rebbe's favorite students. "Chanukah honors those times in our lives when sun and moon, the direct light of God and the reflected light of our tradition are at their nadir. It is a time of trouble, fear and sadness. The work of Chanukah is to dispel darkness with the kindling of lights. That is what we must contemplate throughout these eight days," Chaim said, answering the question the rebbe had forgotten he had asked.

The rebbe nodded his head in approval, grateful to Chaim for reminding him of the inner work to be done.

Ever since Yossi's passing, Sarah's nights had been restless. She woke often, feeling tired and dull. The storm the night before had awakened her with the sound of fierce rain and hail beating against the window. Watching the rain, she had remembered how her mother always said whoever is born or married in the rain will be blessed with *mazel.*

The storm had flooded the classroom at the girl's *cheder* where she taught biblical studies. It had damaged the dilapidated roof and left the floor waterlogged. Her class was moved to her sister Esther's room, where the two classes were combined. The students sat paired together at each desk, giggling. Nevertheless, Sarah was grateful when Esther offered to take over both of their classes so she could take the remainder of the day off, as she was feeling intense cramps from the onset of her period.

It was five months since her husband had died. A childless

widow at twenty-two, she felt her monthly bleeding was now wasted on a barren woman. She returned to the courtyard where she lived just across from her father's house. She climbed the stairs to the small flat she had shared with Yossi. After closing the drapes of her bedroom window, she removed her marriage wig, allowing her lustrous, auburn hair to spill over her shoulders. Undressing from the drab mourning clothes she had worn since Yossi's death, she slid into her warm bed, wearing only her soft, white slip.

Sarah looked at the clock. She had a few hours before she was to bring her father his four o'clock tea. Catching an afternoon nap felt tender and peaceful. She fell deeply asleep, *dreaming she was floating out to sea.*

Late in the afternoon, Jonathan escorted David into Mea Shearim, where bearded men strolled the streets in long black coats and fur hats, with curled locks of hair hanging over their ears. The women were dressed in dark skirts and coats that covered them from the neck down to their clumsy Oxford shoes. Their hair was hidden by tight scarves or identical wigs. Walking separately, segregated from the men, they appeared weary, and old beyond their years.

The Hasidim stared suspiciously at David. His clean-shaven face, short brown jacket, jeans, and loafers screamed "outsider." By their glares, it was obvious they didn't like strangers coming into their neighborhood. Most of them belonged to the ultra-orthodox sect known as the Satmars.

David was repelled by the sight of "these people," and told Jonathan he felt he was visiting a strange planet of clones. He wanted to get out of there right away.

Jonathan was disturbed by his reaction. "David, you know nothing about the Hasidim. Judging them by their appearance? That's so shallow." Trying to put him at ease before meeting the rebbe, Jonathan explained that Reb Eli, although orthodox, did not belong to any sect.

Alone in his study, Reb Eli thought about the promise he had made to his friend, Phillip Bennett. He had known the Bennetts since childhood when his family had sent him to England from his home in Germany.

In November 1938, five days after *Kristalnacht,* the renowned Reb Yaacov Wolfner had decided to send his youngest child, Eliezer, who was almost fifteen, to England through the *Kindertransport,* an organization that rescued Jewish children from Nazi Germany and found them foster homes in England.

"How strange," he thought, "that we forget so easily what we did yesterday, but remember so vividly what the heart felt long ago." It was now nearly thirty years since Reb Eli's last *Shabbat* dinner with his parents and siblings. He remembered his father had invited two young rabbinical students as guests. He could still hear the songs and chants. He could still taste the sweet *challah* bread his mother had baked. He remembered how the *Shabbat* candles had magically turned their home into a haven of peace and beauty; how he had cherished the days when he was able to study alongside his father.

At Berlin's Friedrichstrasse railway station, Reb Yaakov held his son's arm tightly, not saying a word. All around, families were tearing themselves apart, pushing their children into railway carriages under the hostile eyes of the SS, fearing this would be their last time together. Children cried out for their parents even as the train carrying them to England pulled away from the platform.

Several days earlier, his father had explained why he had to leave Germany. He was being sent to England where he would be safe. His father had assured him he would be well cared for, as his friend, the Chief Rabbi of the Emergency Council in England, would place him in a good home. He promised to send for him as soon as the Nazi regime was over and told him always to remember where he came from, and to live by the teachings of the Torah.

When young Eliezer arrived in Harwich he was driven to Hampshire, where the Bennetts took him into their home. He remembered the drive up the long road to their estate, how he stood there staring in awe at the majesty of it all. It was grander than anything he had ever seen. When the Bennett family came out to greet him, he was too intimidated to speak. It was only when their son, Phillip, reached out his hand, that he was able to say hello.

The Bennetts were generous and compassionate secular Jews, careful to keep their philanthropy anonymous, especially all they did for their fellow Jews.

Phillip Bennett and Eliezer were close in age and befriended each other immediately, despite their different enthusiasms. For Eliezer, it was the study of Torah; for Phillip, it was rugby. Their common interest was chess, a game at which Eliezer excelled. When war broke out, they would hike out into the fields in search of German paratroopers, missions which Philip insisted be kept secret from his parents.

Each time they went out, Eliezer would pray they would not run into any Nazis. Other than his fear of Nazis, Eliezer learned to enjoy their outdoor adventures. He loved Hampshire's open, green fields and narrow, gushing streams, often writing to his parents about the English countryside. He looked forward to when they would come for him, so he could show them how beautiful it was. He also let them know the Bennetts had arranged for him to continue his religious studies. Phillip and "Eli,'" as he soon became known, became firm friends.

When the war ended, Eli learned of the fate of his family. They had been taken to Auschwitz and murdered. At twenty years old, he was left orphaned and bereft. He yearned for his family and the life he had known. Germany was no longer a place he could call home. As welcomed as the Bennetts made him feel, and as close as he was to Phillip, Eli desperately needed to return to his own ground. Like so many displaced Jews, he found himself drawn to a new beginning in the Promised Land. In 1946, with the Bennetts support, Eli left for Jerusalem, where he would follow in his father's footsteps and become a rabbi.

During the early, struggling years of the new state of Israel, and through its wars, Phillip had sent generous support, both to Reb Eli, who had started a family, and to the nation. Now, it was Reb Eli's turn to be generous.

He had been taken by surprise when Phillip, who professed to be an atheist, told him of his nephew's desire to learn about Judaism. Jonathan was the son of Eleanor, Phillip's younger sister, whom he knew well from his time in England.

She had married an aristocratic Jew, secular in his ways, yet committed to supporting Israel as insurance against an anti-Semitic world.

Reb Eli had become very fond of Jonathan, though he remained something of an enigma to him. He could not understand how a young man, coming from such wealth, without religious upbringing, could suddenly decide to come to Jerusalem to study Judaism. Was it a rebellion against his family, or was he simply searching for a spiritual path? Or perhaps it had to do with the loss of his father at a young age? Eleanor had told him how much the boy had suffered. For the past three years, Reb Eli had observed Jonathan closely. He appreciated his devotion to his studies, yet remained curious about his motives.

Then, two weeks earlier, Phillip had called asking for help for his only son, David. "My son is lost. He doesn't know where he belongs. He can't seem to find himself. Eli, see what you can do. Jonathan has promised to help as well."

As much as he wanted to help Phillip, he doubted there was much he could do. So many families, especially from America, begged for his help with lost souls. Young people who had no roots were like trees that fall in the first wind. How could he give them the spiritual foundation their families had failed to provide? Most of the time, he could do no more than offer them blessings and prayers. But this was Phillip's son. He owed Phillip so much. This would have to be different. Reb Eli prayed that the hand of God would guide him.

Promptly, at four o'clock, Sarah brought him his tea, with two biscuits. The rebbe's heart ached at his daughter's appearance. Her once sparkling eyes were now dull and empty. She moved like a woman who had been thwarted by life. Lost for words of comfort, the rebbe gently asked his daughter how she was feeling. "I'm fine, Abba," she said quietly, then left to join her sisters in the kitchen to help prepare the evening meal.

"You're on your own now," Jonathan said when they reached the courtyard of the rebbe's house.

"I haven't a clue what to say or what I'm even doing here," David muttered nervously. "Aren't you at least going to introduce us?"

"No need. Just be brave and honest. See you later."

Other than what Jonathan had told him, and his father's story of how he had lived with the family during the war, David knew little about the rebbe, except that he was now the Chief Rabbi of Jerusalem and had remained a close friend of his father.

He felt awkward and out of place knocking at the rebbe's door. A young Hasidic man greeted him and ushered him into Reb Eli's study.

The rebbe was sitting by a large table, facing the door. "Please," he motioned for David to sit across from him in the worn, upholstered chair. Reb Eli's blue eyes were gentle and inquisitive. His head of prematurely white hair and his full salt-and-pepper beard added to David's impression that he was meeting an Old Testament prophet. He sat in the chair and waited for the rebbe to speak, anticipating many questions. Instead, Reb Eli sat silently, periodically closing his eyes in meditation. Not knowing what to say or do, David remained quiet. After a while, a wave of peace washed over him. He became aware of the flow of his breath and the beat of his heart. He heard himself say, "I have so many questions."

"Questions are good, they are all we have, because there are no answers," the rebbe countered in a tone tender enough for a small child.

In the kitchen, Sarah and her sisters had been washing and cutting fresh-bought vegetables, when Esther asked if one of them would mind running to the *macholet* for some garlic. Miriam suggested Sarah should go because she had "had a long rest in the afternoon."

Sarah left for the corner market. Outside the house, in the courtyard, she was looking down when she spotted a pair of brown loafers walking past her. She looked up, curious to see who belonged to these foreign shoes. David, engrossed in his thoughts, walked by without noticing her. Sarah glanced into his face and saw the refined shape of his head, how his hand gently brushed away the dark-brown wisps of hair that had fallen on his forehead. She felt a sudden queasiness in her stomach at noticing so much about a stranger. Trying to dismiss the incident, she rushed to the market, then back to the kitchen where she began mincing the unpeeled garlic cloves until Miriam cried, "Sarah, you forgot to peel the garlic!"

The setting sun covered the city in warm, mellow hues of amber and purple. David was glad he had decided to walk back to Abu Tor. The meeting with the rebbe had left him longing for things he could not name. He was baffled by the rebbe's silence. Why had he not spoken? Was it because Reb Eli sensed he didn't want to be there, or was it just that the rebbe had nothing to say? Perhaps this renowned rebbe was simply bored with one more seeker?

What puzzled David most was why he wanted to see him again. What for? More silence? The rebbe had already told him there were no answers, so what was the point of seeing him again? It would be best to tell Jonathan the meeting had served neither of them well.

At the bottom of the hill at Abu Tor, near the water mill, lay the border between Jordan and Israel, marked by a military post manned by Israeli soldiers. On the other side of the road, Jordanians stood watch at their post. Each monitored the other, day in, day out. Watching the sunset hover over the Old City, David couldn't help but think how bored the soldiers must be, having to stand watch all day, with only each other for company. He saw one of the Jordanians signal for a cigarette. An Israeli soldier put one into a pack and threw it across the road, to a perfect catch. For the moment, their differences dissolved. They became simply two men watching a magnificent sunset, sharing a smoke.

David and Jonathan walked through the ancient tree-lined streets of Baka, a neighborhood of traditional stone houses where Jonathan's girlfriend, Nilli, lived. The houses had been built with Jerusalem stone, a pale limestone with mixed shades of pink, sand and gold that were glowing in the sunset. David admired the buildings and asked where the stones came from.

"They come from local quarries. All houses have to be built with them, by law, to preserve Jerusalem's antiquity. It's why the city is known as Jerusalem of Gold," Jonathan said.

He pried as gently as he could to find out how David's meeting with the rebbe had gone. "He's pretty amazing, isn't he?"

"He said nothing. What's so amazing about that?"

"He doesn't have to say anything. His presence tells you everything you need to know," Jonathan said, trying not to sound preachy.

"Is that it? I just get to sit there in his 'presence'?"

Jonathan laughed. "Didn't you have enough of good conversation in England? I should think by now you would have learned the limitations of language."

"I don't think I will be seeing him again."

"Don't be so quick to judge. It's worth giving it some time," Jonathan said in his older brother tone.

Jonathan was eager for David to meet Nilli and their friends. Feeling out of sorts, David was hesitant about meeting everyone and tried to excuse himself by insisting he was "too grubby" in his jeans and sweater and wasn't properly dressed.

"I wouldn't worry about that. Nobody here bothers about fashion. It's considered gauche," Jonathan boasted, not letting David off the hook.

Arriving at a small stone house with a painted blue door, David was greeted by Nilli. She had a lovely, open face and smile, with bright blue eyes. She embraced David with a warm hug, "Jonathan has told me so much about you."

"I hope some of it was good," David smiled.

Her warmth put him immediately at ease. The door opened into the living room, where three people sat on bright oriental pillows around a large brass coffee table.

Jonathan introduced Nilli's roommate, Anat, and Nilli's brother, Gideon, and his girlfriend, Ronit. Anat and Gideon were dressed in military khaki. They each had an Uzi lying beside them. Gideon shared his sister's eyes and smile. Ronit seemed shy and awkward, traits David later discovered were due to her lack of English. Anat was a sensual beauty, with long blonde hair tied in a ponytail. She spoke English with a perfect British accent. David thought she looked amazing in her army fatigues. Her skirt came just above her knees revealing her shapely legs. The uniform accentuated her slim, curved body. Anat let David know immediately she considered herself smart, tough, and well-informed. When he asked if she had studied in England, she told him "I've never left Israel. I make it my business to learn a language in its proper accent."

"Anat makes it her business to know about everything that interests her," Nilli boasted about her friend.

Jonathan warned him, "Don't be surprised if she knows more about England than we do. Anat is a phenomenon. She reads everything in sight, in four languages, and she's got a photographic memory so she retains all of it. I wouldn't bother challenging her on any subject. It will just make you miserable."

"I shall play it safe then, and keep quiet," David said with good humor.

Anat proceeded to prove to him that everything Nilli and Jonathan had said about her was true. She was not only beautiful, but brilliant and provocative.

The evening continued into the early morning. They had wine with Mediterranean salads, pita bread, olives, cheese, fruit, and nuts. Afterwards, Anat rolled some hashish into a cigarette, offering it to everyone. David, feeling at home with the group, was the only one who accepted. Jonathan had to get up early and left soon after. The rest of them continued talking until three in the morning. They all wanted to know about David's travels and what had brought him to Jerusalem. The hashish relaxed him. He opened up about his adventures, and how Jonathan had persuaded him to come to Jerusalem to meet Reb Eli. Feeling that he had been talking too much about himself, he shifted the conversation.

He learned that Gideon was a high-ranking pilot in the Air Force. Anat was an army lieutenant, an atheist and an archeologist, studying to get her doctorate at the Hebrew University. Ronit was an army code decipherer and Nilli was a medical resident serving in Hadassah Hospital's emergency ward. They were all curious about his meeting with Reb Eli, although none of them were religious. They knew that the rebbe was well-respected and admired for his plain-spokenness about the Torah and the Talmud and was known to be deeply immersed in the teachings of the mystics, which especially interested Gideon.

David didn't know if it was the wine, the hashish, or just the early morning hour that made him feel a deep kinship with these people. Whatever it was, it felt good. Nilli made him promise he would come by whenever he felt the need for company. "Abu Tor is a short walking distance from Baka. You can stop by anytime."

Gideon, who listened more than he had spoken during much of the evening, asked David if he would like to see Jerusalem from the air. He offered to pick him up on Saturday to go flying in a twin-engine Cessna that was available to him from the Air

Force. David eagerly accepted.

The next morning, the phone rang at eight, waking David from a deep sleep. It was Jonathan asking him to meet at Café Cassis.

"I'm a bit sleepy. Didn't get to bed until four. Mind if we meet later?" David mumbled.

"I won't be around later; tied up all day at school. Why don't you get up and nap later? You're on holiday, after all. Come on. I'll have Uri put the kettle on."

David found Jonathan seated at the same table, reading the *Jerusalem Post.*

Uri, the owner, brought over a cup of tea, with a glass of milk on the side. "If you want more tea, I bring you."

"Hungry?" Jonathan asked.

"I think I've had enough of the finely pressed sausage, thank you."

"It's an acquired taste. You'll get there," Jonathan assured him.

"I'm quite happy as I am, thank you," David said, as he removed the tea bag brewing in his cup. "I wish you had told me to bring along some decent tea as well."

"I didn't think there'd be much room left, after the toilet paper. First things first, you know." Jonathan whispered.

"Enjoyed last night," David said, adding a little milk to his tea.

"Good. What do you think of Anat?"

"Smashing."

"Any interest in getting to know her better?" Jonathan

inquired matter-of-factly.

"Not particularly."

"How come?"

"A lady who carries an Uzi is not my idea of a romantic date."

"Don't be absurd. Everyone carries an Uzi here. They all serve in the army."

"I don't, and neither do you," David reminded him.

"You'll get used to it."

"God, I hope not," David moaned. "Seriously, I think Nilli and all your friends are great and lots of fun. I'm just not ready for any sort of romance."

For as long as Jonathan could remember, David was never interested in "romantic entanglements." In England he'd had many girlfriends, but never a steady one. Jonathan decided to let it ride. He was concerned about David and didn't want anything to become a source of friction between them. He was grateful he was in Jerusalem and had met with the rebbe. When Jonathan was growing up, his mother had spoken of Reb Eli with great respect and appreciation, telling him how much he had helped her find the strength to deal with the death of his father. Jonathan was also grateful to the rebbe for taking him under his wing. Reb Eli had become a great inspiration to him, and he hoped the rebbe would be able to help David, too, find his way in the world.

"Well, I'm glad you found Nilli and my friends engaging," Jonathan said, keeping the conversation light and cheerful.

"Gideon has invited me to go flying with him on Saturday."

"Really, that's quite impressive. Gideon is not one for wasting time with insignificant others. Frankly, it took him a year to warm up to me. Must be he took a real liking to you. I have to admit, that makes me feel a bit put out."

"Don't be. I'm not the one sleeping with his sister," David reassured him.

"I take your point. Thank you."

"I like Gideon. I suspect there's a lot more to him than meets the eye."

"There is."

When Sarah brought in her father's afternoon tea, he asked her if she would sit with him for a moment. Pleased to have her father to herself, she sat down on the old, worn chair, the chair she shared with so many others who hungered for his wisdom and guidance. Reb Eli was a man of few words. He never talked much about himself or divulged anything about those who came to see him. Idle talk and gossip were unwelcome. Everyone's confidences were well kept in his inner world, which belonged to him alone. Even Sarah and her siblings knew little about their father's past, other than he had spent several years in England during World War II. Like everything else, details about their father or others were never given or discussed.

He was used to counseling all sorts of people. He had given comfort to so many. It pained him that he could not find a way to reach his own daughter. He sat quietly praying for the right words to come to him.

Sensing her father's concern, Sarah knew the best way to put him at ease was with a direct question. "Why do some people have more difficult lives than others?"

Sarah's question was filled with loneliness and despair. It tore at the rebbe's heart. He spoke to her in his gentle manner. "When it rains, you can shout for the sun, but neither the sun nor the rain will hear you. There is either your acceptance or your rejection. The first leads to peace; the second, to suffering. God pursues you with peace, offering each moment for your appreciation. There is no profit in rejection, but with acceptance comes tranquility and hope for the future."

"How do you find tranquility and hope?" she asked.

"The mysteries are an open secret, Sarah. It is we who must come out of hiding. Some days are bright, others are dark. We should not make a drama of the light, or a tragedy of the dark. Just embrace each as it is, knowing that happiness comes when we live each moment in peace. The whole of life is impermanent; there is no certainty. There's no salvation to lift us out of it, and no reward for suffering. Thinking otherwise is like pursuing the wind. You are a wise and learned woman, Sarah. You know these things. You must try to live them."

"It's not easy, *Abba.*"

"I know," Reb Eli said quietly.

At that moment, Sarah longed to be five years old again, sitting in her father's lap while he gently stroked her hair. Not since she was a child was that permissible. Being observant of the orthodox law, girls over twelve were not permitted to have physical contact with any male, even with their brother or their father. It was forbidden. By twelve, she had lost her mother to cancer, and she had lost her father's physical affection. This would have to come from female family members and friends. The only man once permitted to touch Sarah was her now dead husband. Sarah wished she could find comfort in her father's words, but she could not. Neither could she find solace in her sisters' arms. Her loneliness weighed heavily on her body and her soul. She found comfort only in books. Books were her special friends. She loved the way they opened the outside world to her, leaving her imagination free to dream and experience whatever thoughts and feelings came to visit her. Sarah and her eldest sister, Devorah, kept secret her frequent trips to the library. When Sarah married Yossi, he too became her secret-keeper.

Yossi was not like any of the other young men among the Hasidim. He was more open and willing to give his wife the freedom to seek any knowledge she desired, even if it meant going to the city library alone. Sarah had known Yossi since they were toddlers. As long as Sarah could remember, Yossi and she were good friends. Although she was a girl, Yossi would debate the meanings of the Torah and Mishnah with her. Sarah and Yossi's marriage had been arranged and both were content and agreeable to the match. Their marriage was like their friendship: tender, respectful and loving. Yossi agreed Sarah would not have to cut her beautiful hair, which is expected of married women. Luckily for Sarah, Devorah worked in the *mikveh* where Sarah would always arrive last for the Friday cleansing ritual. With her sister as the only witness, she would neatly tie up her hair, then immerse herself twelve times under the water, in honor of the twelve tribes of Israel. Thereafter, her spirit and body would be cleansed.

Whenever Sarah left home, she would wear the customary *sheitel,* neatly tucking every strand of her own hair under the coarse brown wig, styled with bangs, just like the other married women. At night, Yossi loved to brush her long, thick auburn hair. Then, when it was permissible, they would be intimate. All other times, they slept in their separate twin beds.

Now that Yossi was gone, Sarah knew she had not only lost a husband, but her best friend. She knew no one would be as kind, gentle and accepting of her as Yossi had been. She tried to acquiesce to God's will that she be left childless and alone. She understood the only suitor who would be willing to marry her now would be one of the elderly men who had been widowed, such as Itzhak, the loner across the courtyard, whom she had caught spying on her from his window. Sarah preferred her aloneness to being with someone old enough to be her father.

The rebbe knew his words had failed to soothe his daughter's wounded spirit. He was at a loss. How could he bring comfort to her? All that was left for him was to accept his helplessness about it. He closed his eyes and did what he knew best. He prayed.

His thoughts shifted to David, who would be arriving shortly. He found David to be earnest and sincere. He wished he had come at a better time, when he wasn't so preoccupied with his own concerns. Nevertheless, he would pray and ask *Hashem* to show him a way to reach this lost young man.

For his part, David had made up his mind to challenge the rebbe: no more sitting in silence. If the rebbe had no answers for him, he would not waste his time. He approached Mea Shearim determined to be a force to be reckoned with. He entered the rebbe's study and sat down on the chair with a thud.

"Reb Eli, I've been thinking..."

"So have I," interrupted the rebbe. "How would you like to join me every Thursday evening at eight? You will ask a question each week, then we will contemplate your question, which you will take into consideration until the following week, when you will come in with another question. Do you agree to do this for at least eight weeks?"

As if speaking with someone else's voice, David heard himself mutter, "Yes."

"Good, now take a moment and ask your first question."

David felt himself go blank. "I can't think of one just now."

"Then I have one for you," replied the rebbe. "Why is it a young man like yourself is not married or betrothed?"

Feeling as if he had been knocked off his feet, David tried to catch his balance, and mumbled, "I don't know."

"Do you enjoy being with a woman?"

"Yes, of course...," David answered, nervously, wondering how the rebbe knew he had a problem. His shameful secret must be written all over his face, he thought. Every time David got intimate with a woman, he would ejaculate prematurely. Each relationship added to his humiliation and left him feeling more inept than before. David would repeatedly tell himself he would do better next time. Next time always proved to be the same. The women were just as embarrassed by his predicament as he was. They would ignore it as though nothing had happened, as if that would ease his shame. To avoid any further distress, he always found an amicable excuse for breaking off the relationship. Confronted by the rebbe, David sat quietly for some time. Reb Eli waited patiently, giving him the time he needed to gather the courage to speak. "I have trouble holding myself," he confessed, in a whisper.

The rebbe was as astounded about his inquiry as was David. He had no idea why he had asked that particular question, and was just as amazed when he heard the answer come out of David's mouth. Feeling this was divine intervention, he offered David the only assistance he could muster. "Can you be here Sunday evening at eight?"

From her bedroom window, Sarah spotted David walking across the courtyard, wearing the same brown loafers and jacket. Once again, she felt an odd twinge in her stomach. What was this modern man, dressed in European clothes, doing in Mea Shearim? Perhaps he was visiting a distant relative? There were several Hasidim who were visited by outsiders, but not often. This was the second time in two weeks she had seen him. She became preoccupied with what he was doing in Mea Shearim, and wondered why he should have such a peculiar effect on her. Then she caught herself and dismissed her thoughts as idle nonsense, caused by her unsettled state. She felt like a stranger to herself and a burden to her family. Nothing made sense to her anymore.

Every Friday night, all twenty-five members of the rebbe's family gathered for *Shabbat.* They would sit in their customary places at the *Shabbat* tables, Sarah with her three sisters, her two sisters-in-law, and their children at one table; Reb Eli at the head of the men's table with his two sons and sons-in-law and his three eldest grandsons. His eldest daughter, Dvorah, would light the *Shabbat* candles as the women covered their eyes and chanted the prayer welcoming the *shechinah,* the peace of the *Shabbat* bride, to their home and heart. At the conclusion of each *Shabbat,* the rebbe's grandchildren would line up before him and he would place his hands over each of their heads for a special blessing.

Sarah felt bereaved. She would never bring forth a child for her father's blessing. She was aware how her sisters, who knew of her anguish, avoided looking into her eyes.

At the end of the meal, Reb Eli gave Sarah a nod, her cue to start singing. Nothing pleased him more than the sound of Sarah's voice. It created a peace that filled the room and touched his soul. Afterwards, the children sang traditional Sabbath songs, with all of the family joining in.

As the women cleared the table, Sarah heard Reb Eli ask her brother, Yaacov, to arrange for Shimon to come see him. She knew summoning Shimon meant a visit to the "House." She wondered which of the young men was having personal issues and needed help.

After *Shabbat,* she went back to her flat. Since Yossi's death, she had stopped going to the weekly *mikveh.* She preferred, instead, to light her own *Shabbat* candles, carefully placing them on the windowsill from where she could watch them flicker while she enjoyed her meditation. But tonight, her thoughts flowed to the first time she had followed her brother, Isaac, to the House. She remembered how her mother had wept copiously at the dining room table, the night Isaac was caught caressing his best friend, Moshe, in the shower of the men's *mikveh.* Her mother, who was weakened by illness, had pleaded with her father to "have Shimon take Isaac to the House." When her father refused, she begged until he became weary with guilt. Seeing the fragility of his wife, he could not deny her and, despite his reservations, arranged for Isaac to be taken there. Sarah had just turned twelve and wondered why it was so wrong for her brother to have shown affection for Moshe. She was also curious about the House and why Isaac had to go there.

The previous week there had been so much whispering between her parents that it piqued her curiosity so much that she decided to follow her brother and Shimon, secretly, keeping her distance. She watched them enter a house in the heart of Machane Yehuda's open souk on Agripas Street, the main market in Jerusalem, which was a short distance from Mea Shearim, and deserted at night.

Her first glimpse of Madame Aziza was from a bench across the street where she sat looking up at the balcony, through panes of glass doors and windows that were draped with white laced curtains. She could see the silhouette of a woman who was elaborately dressed. It would be years before she learned who she was.

The lights from the House sparkled against the darkness of the night. When scantily dressed young women with flowing, bright scarves appeared, Sarah became mesmerized and watched spellbound as they danced sensually before Isaac. She watched her brother go off with one of the girls, but couldn't see where they had gone, or what they were doing. She imagined the girl would dance for Isaac and, if he were nice to her, she would let him kiss her so he wouldn't have to caress Moshe anymore and make her mother cry.

After that night, Sarah imagined she, too, could dance with beautiful scarves in the same graceful way that would please men. Thereafter, whenever she heard about one of the young men having a personal problem who needed a visit to the House, Sarah would wait until her sisters were asleep, then dress and escape into the night and walk the narrow streets to Madame Aziza's house to watch from the bench and marvel at the exotic dancing of the young women.

It was during that time that Sarah's life changed forever. Her mother had been struggling with her illness for years. Watching her slip into the hands of death became unbearable. Toward the end, she and her brothers and sisters would take turns looking after her. Each afternoon, from two until four, her father would be with her. At night, when everyone was asleep, Sarah took to escaping to the privacy of her father's study to lock out the world and pretend to be one of Madame Aziza's dancing enchantresses. Alone, in the solitude of her imagination, she, too, became a beautiful dancer. She imagined being married, dancing to the delight of her husband, and giving him many sons, which would please *Hashem* who, perhaps, would spare her mother from dying. Sarah's secret world was not to be shared with anyone.

God did not spare her mother. And at fourteen she discovered the truth about what was going on in the House. Her sister, Esther, explained that her husband, Yitzhak, was having difficulty performing his husbandly duties, so it was arranged for him to be taken to Madame Aziza's house. Esther was not happy with the arrangement, but Yitzhak's problem was keeping her from conceiving. She told Sarah that men went to Madame Aziza's house where they paid women to help them overcome such problems. Sarah was shocked and embarrassed by how stupid she had been not to realize that Madame Aziza's was a house of prostitution. She feared what her sisters would think if they knew she had been sneaking out after dark to watch and enjoy harlots dancing, imagining herself to be one of them.

Lying in bed, Sarah wondered if Isaac, with his four sons and two daughters, and her sister Esther, with her three sons and two daughters, were grateful to Madame Aziza. It was only she who was left devoid of children and without a husband. Perhaps this was *beshert* for having secretly stolen away to live vicariously as one of Madame Aziza's seductresses.

Flying high above Jerusalem at sunrise, David looked out of the window of the Cessna, spellbound by the glistening light that bathed the city. "It's magnificent," he said.

Gideon smiled proudly, as though Jerusalem belonged to him personally. "For thousands of years, so many have fought over her."

"Her?" asked David.

"Do you know of another city that has given birth to three such religions?"

"No, thank heaven. I imagine it would just cause more conflict and wars."

"Perhaps, but none would be as Jerusalem."

Gideon circled lower, giving David a closer view of the curving domes, soaring minarets, and the Western Wall of the Temple.

"There's the Old City."

"Do you think there's any chance of peace?"

"That's a question for our neighbors."

"Surely they believe in peace?"

"They're too afraid democracy and education will corrupt them, especially their women. Liberated women are their worst nightmare. Our own orthodox have the same problem."

Gideon pointed into the distance, "Over there is Hebron. It's where our patriarchs are buried."

David asked, "Do you really think that's what it's about for the Arabs? Not wanting their women to be liberated?"

"Mostly. With the Christians it's different. With them, we are a constant reminder that even though their God was born and died a Jew, we don't go along with their story." Gideon was quiet for a moment. "I believe that's why they found it easy to kill six million of us."

"You can't blame the Christians for what the Nazis did."

"And who were the Nazis before Hitler came along?"

"What about the Christians who helped save Jews?"

"Too bad the Pope wasn't one of them."

"The world has changed. You have your own country now."

"Exactly, and we intend to keep it. Do you really believe being British excludes you from being a Jew?"

"Frankly, I've never given it much thought."

"Being Jewish is not something the world will allow you to opt out of."

David felt he had been insensitive and wanted to explain himself. "I've never had any desire to be part of a tribe. I think each of us has to find his own way in the world. I just wish I could find mine."

David was pushed back in his seat as Gideon pointed the plane skywards.

"I understand," said Gideon as he turned the Cessna upside down into a roll.

David felt his stomach rise to his chest. Queasy, he began gagging.

"Being in the world without roots, and not belonging somewhere, is like flying through life upside down," Gideon said evenly, turning the Cessna back over.

"I see what you mean," David said, grateful to have his stomach and equilibrium back in place.

"Feeling better?"

"Sort of."

Tsipi's was a dive in a back alley in the heart of town. Most of the people there on this Saturday night were young Israelis, drinking with friends, or dancing to their version of a rock band. The air was rank with cigarette smoke and David's throat became irritated. He ordered a beer to soothe it. It was dark and tasted of malt.

Anat seemed to know everyone there and introduced David as "my friend from England." She was dressed in a dark blue mini-dress, which David thought was nearly as seductive as her army uniform. He wondered if he had been set up to go dancing with her. Earlier in the evening, everyone had an excuse for not joining them. Jonathan and Nilli said they were too tired; Gideon and Ronit had to get an inhaler from the pharmacy for Ronit's mother, who was sick with bronchitis.

Anat was a good dancer and made sure everyone knew it. She seemed to know every move he was going to make. Her body was right there, in rhythm with him. David wondered if she desired him as much as he did her. He suspected she had dressed up to impress him, which flattered him. He tried to keep up with her dancing until he felt weak with hunger, as he hadn't eaten since lunch. He asked if she knew where they could get something to eat. She suggested Mickey's. "It's the only place open at night that serves good food."

Mickey's was a small, crowded restaurant with bare Formica tables. A couple had just finished eating and were leaving when they walked in. Anat introduced David to the proprietor, Mickey, a burly forty-year-old Syrian Jew who could barely speak English. By the way they spoke rapidly in Hebrew, it was obvious they knew each other very well, and shared a warm friendship. Mickey was a charismatic man with a hearty laugh. David felt an immediate liking for him. Within minutes, Mickey, who was also the cook, brought out salads, warm pita bread, chicken and lamb kabobs. Everything was delicious. Anat ate and drank like no one David had ever seen. She was insatiable. For dessert, she ate three flans that she washed down with three cups of Turkish coffee. Finally, David burst out laughing.

"What is it?"

"You eat like a bloody horse. I've never seen anything like it. Where does it all go?"

"I've been this way all my life. I just burn it off. In an hour, I'll probably be hungry again." She licked her lips, continuing to devour the last of her third flan.

"She eat always like this. Where it go, I don't know," Mickey said, laughing.

Walking through the city toward Abu Tor, the streets were empty and still. In the distance, near the windmill, all that could be seen were the lit cigarettes of the sentries at the border post, flickering like lightening bugs.

Given the provocative way Anat had danced, David thought she would expect to be invited up to his place. Although he desired her, her heightened energy made him anxious. He feared he was not up to dealing with her.

"How was flying with Gideon?"

"Amazing. I don't believe I will ever forget it. He has quite a way of making his point," David admitted.

Anat laughed, "So you've discovered Israeli men don't have your refined manners?"

"Yes. I've gathered as much."

Arriving at the house in Abu Tor, Anat simply followed him up the stairs to his flat, in continuation of their walk. There was no need for an invitation.

David tried to hide his nervousness by asking her if she was still hungry.

"I might be a horse, but I'm not a cow. Do you have any hash?"

"Jonathan made me promise not to bring any. He said I would be deported if I got caught with it."

Anat laughed. "Jonathan takes his Judaic studies too seriously. He might find God sooner if he smoked some himself."

"I have a bottle of wine, compliments of Jonathan. Would you like some?"

"Sure."

While he searched for a bottle opener, Anat opened the doors to the roof, looking out at the city. "Great view. It's a bit chilly, but do you mind if we have our wine out here?" she asked.

"Not at all. It's the best room in the house."

He brought out the bottle with two glasses. He poured Anat a full glass, his, only a third, as he had already had several beers at Tsipi's.

"It's bad luck not to have a full glass," she teased.

"Only if your intentions are to pass out."

Anat pointed toward Jaffa Road, a wide, winding road below the King David Hotel. "There's Gai Ben-Hinnom where Jews, Muslims and Christians believe, on Judgment Day, the Gates of Hell will open and devour all us sinners with fire. It's one of the few things they all agree on." She pointed to the far distance, at the left. "Over there is the archaeological park. I was there today, on a dig."

"Find anything interesting?"

"Only if you find used prophylactics interesting."

"Could be, if they belonged to Moses or Jesus."

"Two of history's most sexually repressed men," Anat replied, dryly.

"How do you know that?"

"Jesus, alias Yehoshua Ben Joseph, and Moses were both Jews who would have followed the tribe's sexual laws."

The wine was warming David, taking the chill off the night air. Amused by her audacity, he coaxed her on. "All right, but how do you know they were sexually repressed."

Anat shot him a look. "Do you honestly believe a man who had great sex would bother running around trying to convince everybody he was the only Son of God, or had personally received God's hand-written laws on top of a mountain?"

"Why not? Men can have ambitions as well as desires."

"Not when they're having great sex."

David suddenly felt challenged. He stood staring out into the night.

As though she could read his mind, Anat said, "Don't worry, we're not going to sleep together."

David looked at her, not knowing what to say or expect.

"At least not tonight. I like men, but prefer women," she said, shrugging.

He didn't know whether to feel rejected or relieved.

David lay awake thinking about Anat. He was intimidated by her sexuality, but also fascinated by her free spirit and daunting intelligence. He had never met anyone like her. He wondered if Jonathan and the others knew she preferred women lovers, and why she had confided in him. He became anxious, thinking perhaps she sensed he had sexual issues and was someone she could easily manipulate.

Earlier, out on the roof, he had asked her why she preferred women. She had answered simply, "For the same reasons you do," then adding, "I find women more interesting intellectually, as well as sexually."

Her directness was equal parts frightening and exciting. He wanted to know her better. Perhaps, with her, he could get over his sexual problem. The truth was, he desired her as much as he found her intimidating.

The streets in Mea Shearim were busy on Sunday afternoon, when the shops re-opened after the long Shabbat. The men hurried about their business while the women shopped for the coming week.

The last rays of daylight came through Sarah's bedroom window. She had been reading Martin Buber's *I and Thou* throughout the Sabbath and couldn't pull herself away from it. She pondered Buber's premise that man separates himself from God when he views himself as "I" and others as "Thou." Reb Eli had a great affinity for Buber's work. His books were among the few non-religious volumes he kept in his extensive library. Sarah also loved Isaac Bashevis Singer's stories about Jewish life in Poland, and the heart-rending dilemmas faced by his characters. Singer had no illusions about the human condition, nor did he offer simple, happy endings. He presented the complexity and relentless challenge of being human, something she, too, had come to understand.

Just as it became dark, Sarah spotted a man striding purposefully into the courtyard. She immediately recognized him as the outsider who had aroused in her such unusual sensations. She moved closer to the window, hiding behind the heavy curtains so she could study him more carefully. She was able to see the angular features of his face, and, again, the way his hand swept the hair from his forehead. When she saw him enter her father's house, she immediately sensed he was the reason for the rebbe's summoning of Shimon. She was intrigued by this outsider. Where did he come from? Why would a secular man require a visit to the House? Sarah knew she lived in a confined religious society, and that there were many things she didn't know about the outside world, beyond what she read in books. Her curiosity heightened as she waited by the bedroom window, in anticipation of seeing Shimon escort the stranger to Madame Aziza's house.

Shimon stood five feet, two inches tall and had a big round belly and wispy red hair and beard. David thought he looked like an Irish elf. A man of good cheer, Shimon took his mission of performing *mitzvahs* like that of a general who had been given orders to lead his troops to victory. David was a new recruit who was about to assume his God-given, manly duty of bringing children into the world. Shimon, as the liaison with Madame Aziza's house, discharged his task with honor and pride. He was most eager that David, the son of a friend of the rebbe's, should benefit from his good deeds. Shimon's English was limited, so to demonstrate his sincerity, in hopes of gaining David's confidence and trust, he stood up and enthusiastically embraced David as soon as he entered the rebbe's study.

David instinctively pulled back. Shimon's goodwill gesture embarrassed him. David's eyes pleaded for Reb Eli's help. The rebbe rose and said simply, "This is my nephew, Shimon. He will take good care of you. Until Thursday. I wish you a good night."

Bewildered, David stood looking at Shimon, who was smiling, saying repeatedly, "Don't worry, everything good, everything good."

He followed him apprehensively through the dark, narrow

streets of Machane Yehuda's Souk to the two-story stone house on Agripas Street. Shimon, still smiling, opened the door, ushering him in. Climbing the pitch-dark staircase, he cautioned David to "be careful, just count twenty steps."

On the second landing, Shimon knocked briskly on the door. A woman in her late fifties appeared. She had long dark hair, with coal-black eyes. She reminded David of the fortune-tellers who roam India. Shimon introduced him to Madame Aziza, who graciously invited them in.

Burgundy velvet drapes with gold tassels adorned the windows of her parlor. A gold-leaf tapestry covered the walls. On the floor were oriental carpets in deep reds, blues and gold. The largest had corners containing dragons with snakes around their necks. David wondered whether this woman was going to read his fortune or perform some magic healing ritual that would keep him from coming every time he was aroused by a woman. Speaking in a soft, melodic voice, her well-spoken English was colored with French and Arabic accents. She offered them drinks from her cabinet of wine and spirits. Shimon requested Turkish coffee. To keep it simple and quick, David asked for the same.

Madame Aziza made polite conversation, inquiring where David was from. He told her he was visiting from England. She asked him if he was married or divorced. He said neither, wondering why all this concern about his marital status. He began thinking perhaps she was a matchmaker, when a young, exotic looking woman with red lips and nails appeared from the kitchen, carrying a brass tray with a *finjan* of dark black coffee and an assortment of small pastries. She served them with her eyes locked into David's, then quickly disappeared. Shimon helped himself to the sticky pastries, which had the scent of cardamom. David slowly nursed the muddy coffee. Sensing he was not a Turkish coffee drinker, Madame Aziza offered him "English tea."

David assured her he was fine with coffee.

Madame Aziza looked curiously at him. "You're a handsome young man."

Feeling self-conscious, David replied, timidly, "Thank you."

"Please help yourself to some pastries. They're very tasty."

Accepting her offer, he reached for one with nuts in it. Feeling like the center of attention, he ate self-consciously.

Shimon sat grinning from ear to ear. He sipped the remains of his coffee, informed David that the number four bus across the souk on Jaffa Road would drop him off at Abu Tor, then left abruptly.

Soft, Middle Eastern dance music filled the room. Madame Aziza's eyes flashed as she turned to an opening door and said, "Now, for your pleasure."

From a narrow hallway, four young women floated into the room and began dancing. David sat mesmerized, not knowing what to do. He watched as they danced before him, swaying their hips, shoulders and arms like slithering snakes.

Madame Aziza put her hand gently on his shoulder. "Let me know when you decide which one pleases you the most."

Finding it difficult to believe that Reb Eli had sent him to a whorehouse, David asked incredulously, "Is this a bordello?"

Madame Aziza smiled. "This is a house that nurtures men's passions and desires."

"I'm really not ready for this," he admitted awkwardly.

"There is nothing to be ready for, just relax and enjoy," she said, gently reassuring him.

"If you don't mind, I'd like to take some time to consider your generous offer."

Her voice took on a motherly tone. "There is nothing to fear here."

"I'm sure. It's just that I would like to think about it," he said, adamantly.

Madame Aziza looked at him in her nurturing fashion. "You may visit us whenever you are ready. I will make sure you have the very best. I desire only what is good for your happiness."

"Thank you," David said, as he quickly left.

Walking along the Mount, near the University of Jerusalem, Jonathan howled with laughter. "The rebbe never ceases to amaze me. Why on earth did he send you to a brothel?"

David could not bring himself to reveal his sexual issues, but when Jonathan went on and on questioning why Reb Eli would send him to a whorehouse, David felt compelled to tell him.

"Because I told him I come too quickly," David whispered.

Astonished, Jonathan repeated David's words, "You told the rebbe you come too quickly?"

"Yes."

"Why did you tell him that?"

"Because it's true."

Seeing that this was no laughing matter for David, Jonathan quickly changed his tone. "Why haven't you ever told me?"

"What could you do about it?"

"Surely there are remedies ..."

"There are no 'remedies,' so spare me any advice," David said, becoming irritated.

"I'm sorry, I didn't mean to be insensitive. I just wish ..."

"There's nothing you or anybody else can do. It's something I have to live with."

They walked on quietly around the Mount, looking out at the city.

"Look, David, perhaps if you had a steady girlfriend, it would just work itself out," Jonathan offered, gently.

"What makes you think I haven't thought of that?" David snapped.

Jonathan adopted an apologetic tone. "I don't mean to be intrusive. I really want to help... For God's sake, we've been closer than brothers."

"Then let it be!"

They continued walking in an uncomfortable silence. David felt humiliated and angry, emotionally naked now that his long-kept secret had been exposed.

Remembering the Rebbe's invitation and hoping to break the silence, Jonathan cheerfully announced, "Reb Eli has invited us for *Shabbat* dinner at his home."

Going to the rebbe's house for dinner was the last thing David wanted to do. He moaned, "Oh, joy."

"I think you're making more of it than it really is. I'm sure, given time, it will sort itself out." Jonathan said, hoping to put David at ease.

David felt the remark was flippant. "How easy to say when

it's not your problem."

Madame Aziza has helped many young men. Why should I be opposed to that?" said the rebbe. David looked at him in disbelief. Seeking help in a bordello just didn't sit right with him. Perhaps these Hasids were comfortable with it, but he certainly was not.

Feeling the need to challenge Reb Eli, David argued, "It's not a very holy approach."

"When I first arrived here, I felt the same way. But when I saw how much she helped someone close to me, I came to a different understanding. After all, women who choose to sell their bodies come from the same source as you and I. They are just as holy as we are. The Torah tells us that to give pleasure is a *mitzvah*, but it is silent on how we should do it. It just tells us the no nos."

The rebbe had done it again. "I'm sorry. I didn't mean to imply that I was holier or superior to anyone. It's just that using a woman that way doesn't feel right."

"One should never use another. The Torah teaches us to be kind and honor everyone, not just people we like or respect. There are things we can never know or understand about each other. The Torah recognizes this and gives us principles to live by that cultivate our happiness and wellbeing."

Reb Eli muttered something in Hebrew, and then translated. " There is nothing on this earth that has not been here before or will not be here again.' Do you know where that proverb comes from?"

David shook his head, humbly.

"King Solomon."

"I know nothing of the Torah," David admitted.

"You have the rest of your life to learn," Reb Eli said, his eyes twinkling with warmth. He stood, cupped David's hand into his, and smiled, "I hope you will honor us at our *Shabbat* table tomorrow evening."

Looking out of her window, an hour before she was to bring tea to her father, Sarah saw David approaching for the second time in a week. Her curiosity heightened, she told herself she would go down to the kitchen, ostensibly to get a head start preparing the evening meal.

She could hear murmuring from her father's study. To get closer, she decided to set the large table in the dining room, which was adjacent to the kitchen. As she carefully laid out the dishes, paper napkins and utensils, she could hear David's voice. Making as little noise as possible, she was able to distinguish his British accent, which she found more eloquent than her father's. She was enthralled by the tone and gentleness of his voice, and moved closer to the door, listening as he spoke of his reservations and concerns about going to Madame Aziza's house. She found herself comforted by his direct but gentle manner of speaking. She continued to listen, unaware she was holding her breath. By the time she heard her father invite David for *Shabbat* dinner, she felt queasy and dizzy. She rushed to the kitchen and squeezed a fresh lemon into a glass of water to revive herself.

Soon after David left, Sarah made certain not to look her father in the eye when she brought tea with milk and biscuits into his study. Sensing something was amiss with his daughter,

Reb Eli invited her to join him for tea.

"I've left the potatoes boiling on the stove," she said, hoping to excuse herself.

He asked if she would turn the stove off, then come and join him for a moment. There was something important he wanted to discuss with her. Sarah anxiously obeyed and returned to the study, fearing the rebbe had discovered her eavesdropping.

"Sarah, how would you like to go abroad for a holiday?"

The offer was so unexpected, she responded by asking directly, "Why?"

"You've always had a desire to travel. I thought a trip to Europe would please you. I can arrange for you to stay with good friends of mine and perhaps, if you like, Esther could join you."

Feeling guilty and embarrassed at having just spied on her father's private conversation, Sarah did not know what to say, and answered without looking at him. "Please don't worry about me Abba, I'll be all right."

Reb Eli was left once again feeling at a loss with his daughter. He prayed every morning and night for guidance, assuring himself, "Everything comes with time and patience."

Alone in his study, the rebbe sipped tea, which he always found soothing. He was grateful to the British for teaching him the simple pleasure of a good cup of tea. He thought about Phillip's son, David, whose intelligence and sensitivity were more heightened than in most of the young men he had counseled. He remembered the many times Madame Aziza had been effective in helping them overcome difficulties they had with their sexuality. At first, he had dismissed having anything to do with her. He knew the complexities of human nature and doubted it was possible to change the focus of desire. It wasn't until she helped his youngest son to be willing to marry and have children that he learned to appreciate her gifts. He, himself, had never met her and knew little about her, other than that she had brought with her from Egypt wondrous secrets for awakening and healing the senses of complex young men.

A more pressing matter from Egypt was on his mind. Abdel Nasser's inflammatory speeches and the escalation of raids against Israel made him fear that another war was imminent. He prayed *Hashem* would remember how long the Jews had suffered, how long they had been exiled from their Promised Land. He prayed to *Hashem* to bestow peace and awaken the hearts of all of Abraham's children.

TWO

Sarah lay restless in bed. She dwelled on the Englishman and the prospect of his coming to *Shabbat.* It was customary for her father to invite male guests for *Shabbat.* They would join him at his table, among the male members of the family. Over the years, there were many who had come, mostly religious scholars, from all over the world. She had barely noticed any of them. Why, then, did this secular Englishman stir up such unsettling feelings?

On nights when Sarah could not sleep, she would recite the bedtime prayer before allowing her fingers to open to a random page from the *Tanakh,* believing the hand of *Hashem* would guide her to find the words that would bring insight and comfort for her troubles. She would study and contemplate the deeper meaning of the opened text to gain wisdom and direction for her deepest needs. Tonight, she once again reached for the *Tanakh,* quietly muttered her prayer, and opened the book, at random. She found herslf reading the story of Tamar.

Tamar, like Sarah, lost her husband at an early age and was left childless. According to religious law, she had to wait for an arranged marriage to her husband's eldest available brother. After years of waiting, Tamar was ignored by her husband's family and was left to live the remaining years of her life alone. Feeling thwarted by them, she decided, in her desperation, to pose as a harlot and seduce her father-in-law into impregnating her with his seed, a seed which came from the same source as her deceased husband.

Sarah was bewildered. She wondered what message was to be learned from the story. Was *Hashem* trying to tell her that she, too, was thwarted by life? She thought about her dead husband. Yossi had been an only son, with five sisters. Surely God didn't mean for her to seduce her father-in-law? Was there another member of Yossi's family she was supposed to engage with? The parallel between her and Tamar was too strong a coincidence to ignore. She suddenly felt overwhelmed and exhausted. She kissed the *Tanakh,* as always, before setting it down on her bedside table. She prayed *Hashem* would grant her clarity, and then fell into a deep sleep.

It had rained all night and morning, and was still drizzling as David walked up Ben Yehuda Street, yearning for a hot cup of tea to ward off the chill of the cold, damp air. He headed toward Café Cassis, hoping he might find Jonathan there. It was Friday afternoon, the day Jonathan got off early from his studies.

The café was packed. Gideon and Ronit were sitting in the back at one of the small tables. When Gideon saw him, he motioned for David to join them and quickly pulled a chair from another table for him.

"I hope I'm not imposing," David said, apologetically.

Ronit's smile told him he was welcomed.

"Joining friends is always good. What will you drink?" asked Gideon.

"Tea with milk, please."

Gideon got Uri's attention and placed the order.

"I was hoping to find Jonathan here."

"He and Nilli will be here shortly."

"How are you enjoying Jerusalem?" Ronit inquired.

"Fine, just fine. A few surprises now and again," David replied, keeping his adventures with Gideon and Madame Aziza to himself.

"Jonathan mentioned you've been to see the rebbe. How is it going?" Gideon asked.

"Interesting. He is an insightful man."

"Are you learning about the Kabbalah or is he just trying to make a good Jew of you?"

"Neither that I'm aware of," David said, half-jokingly, as Jonathan and Nilli approached.

Although the table was tight for five, they all squeezed in, huddling together. Jonathan was happy to see David, and quickly joined in the conversation, asking how everyone was doing.

Gideon said he was off to a six-week special training course in the north.

Jonathan asked what that meant. Gideon said he had no idea, which David found difficult to believe. How could someone be sent to a special training course and not know what it's for, or what it's about?

Anat came dashing into the café like a thunderbolt. She greeted everyone, giving David a big hug and kiss on the cheek. She grabbed a chair and seated herself beside him. David felt flattered by her show of affection. Everyone was now crunched together at the table. The intimacy felt good to him.

After the exchange of greetings and ordering of drinks, Anat, in a playful mood, asked, "What's everyone doing for *Shabbat* tonight?"

"David and I have been invited to the rebbe's house," Jonathan boasted.

David, certain Nilli was joining them, wondered why Jonathan had forgotten to mention her. "Isn't Nilli joining us?"

Nilli smiled affectionately at David.

Anat leaned toward him, "Your naïveté about the orthodox is so charming."

"You need to be married or engaged in order to be invited as a couple," Jonathan explained.

Gideon, eager to share his resentment toward the orthodox, joined in. "They like to keep up appearances. It would be nice if they did something useful, like serve in the army, and not just sit back and tell us how to run the country."

"Gideon doesn't appreciate their chutzpah," Anat explained.

"They have nothing to do with what the rebbe is about," Jonathan interrupted. "The rebbe has a responsibility to uphold and abide by traditions. Laying all this political stuff on him is unfair. He's a pious Jew who practices the Torah, as opposed to most who just read it."

"Good, so long as he sticks to his job and leaves us to ours, he has my blessing," Gideon said, pointedly.

Anat, growing bored with the subject, said flatly, "it doesn't matter what we think about them. They're going to become more and more influential because they breed like rabbits." She abruptly switched to boasting about her plans for the evening. "I, like all the other decadent Jerusalemites, will be happily spending the evening at Tsipi's, the only place open on Shabbat,"

"I'm sorry you won't be joining us Nilli," David said earnestly.

"Actually, I couldn't have joined you, I'm on night duty at the hospital, but I would very much like to meet the rebbe."

"Why haven't you ever told me that?" Jonathan said, surprised.

"I just did," Nilli smiled, kissing his cheek.

Standing at the kitchen sink. Sarah tried to keep her knees and hands from trembling as she arranged the platter of sweetened whitefish. She prayed *Hashem* would help her stay calm through the evening so no one would notice her uneasiness.

When she first entered the dining room, she noticed the way David tipped his head from side to side as he was talking with her father. She could see how deep and intense his blue eyes were. She quickly lowered her head, afraid her nervousness would be noticed. She placed the platter before her father and his two guests. Returning to the women's table, she sat beside her three sisters. She kept looking down throughout the evening, avoiding any eye contact with David. She had seen Jonathan before at one of her father's seminars and several times a few years ago when he would visit her father in his study. As a religious woman, she was used to men ignoring her presence. Tonight, she prayed for it, grateful for the *Shabbat* blessing, when she could cover her face with her hands in prayer.

She had dressed carefully for this evening. Her black mourning dress was pressed precisely and her bobbed *sheitel* with bangs was combed to make certain the wig lay tightly against her head without revealing any strands of her hair. She blended in with the women in her family and was confident she was invisible before their English guests.

During the meal, the men talked, while the women served. Sarah was careful not to be caught watching David, while she stole every glance at him that she could. She watched how elegantly he ate, how his long fingers gracefully handled the knife and fork, his boyish smile, and the way he shyly bit his lower lip when amused.

Sitting next to Dvorah, she was in direct view of him when she began to sing. Soon the children, the rebbe and everyone else joined in the songs. She noticed David seemed estranged, far away in his own thoughts. Perhaps if she were not a Hasidic widow, dressed in mourning clothes, the Englishman would have noticed her. Sarah quickly reprimanded herself for having such nonsensical thoughts, *I am who I am,* she silently told herself. From the depths of her soul, she felt an unbearable loneliness. She wished she were elsewhere, far, far away from this, the only life she knew.

After dinner with the rebbe, Jonathan left to see Nilli at the hospital. David decided to meet up with Anat at Tsipi's. By the time he arrived there, Tsipi's was filled with smoke, the smell of hashish thick in the air. After a half hour, he asked Anat if they could leave.

It was drizzling outside. He found it refreshing, after the haze of smoke inside Tsipi's. Anat was eager to know how his evening had gone at the rebbe's house. He confided how baffled he was by the Hasidim. He could not understand why women and men of the same family could not sit together. "The way they dress makes them look like clones. It's difficult to tell them apart."

"If God cared so much about couture, he would have instructed Moses with an eleventh commandment. Thou shalt dress only in drab."

"I don't believe Reb Eli has much interest in couture. Aside from all the ritual, I really enjoyed my conversation with him. And it was lovely when one of the women sang. I don't know who she was, but it was beautiful."

By the time they reached the windmill, it had stopped drizzling. The city was covered in fog and its lights were barely visible.

"Does your family observe Shabbat?"

David laughed. "No. In my family, we confine ourselves to the daily mundanities. There are never any unbecoming expressions of devotion. Meals are usually bland affairs, prepared by the cook, under the direction of my mother, whose main requirement is that the food be prepared in a manner which will keep her looking slim and fit."

"You have a cook? Are you that rich?"

Speaking, or being explicit, about money made David uneasy. It was considered vulgar among the British upper class. Knowing she, as an Israeli, would find his reluctance off-putting and snobbish, he said light-heartedly, "I hope you won't hold it against me."

Anat had never known anyone who was wealthy. "I have always wondered how the rich live, how they were different from the rest of us."

"Wealth provides you with creature comforts and opportunities most people don't have. Sometimes, if you're not careful, you can become estranged from others, and, I'm afraid, quite boring."

"That's one problem we don't have here," Anat said, seriously, "at least not yet."

As she listened to him, it was clear how distanced he felt from his own family, and she heard the loneliness it caused him. She looked at him, her gaze unflinching, "What is it you're hoping to find here?"

"Frankly, I'm not sure. Perhaps some sort of escape."

"From what?"

"From myself, I suppose."

They walked silently through Baka toward Anat's house. Friday nights in Jerusalem were filled with a stillness which intensified David's loneliness. He yearned to get to know Anat more intimately and discover what, if anything, she wanted from him. "Do the others know about your sexuality?" he asked, wanting to know if it was just he whom she trusted enough to confide in.

"They never asked, just assumed I was like most Israeli girls, wanting to get married, have babies and spend the rest of my life yearning for something more."

"I don't think you're like most girls anywhere on the planet."

"Should I take it that you find me unique, or just odd?" Her question was direct. He knew it required an equally direct answer.

"I find you a delightfully unique woman, one I'd like to get to know better."

"Does that include making love to me?" she asked, frankly.

"I have to admit I've given it some thought, accompanied by

a bit of terror."

She laughed heartily. "You needn't be afraid of me. I've appointed you my truest friend and confidant, a much more lasting position than a lover."

He didn't know whether to feel flattered or discarded.

"Now that you are my knight of honor, you must always tell me the truth about yourself."

He trusted her desire for friendship, something he knew he needed as well, yet he couldn't help feeling that perhaps she could help him overcome his problem with women.

"You don't have to be afraid of revealing anything to me, nothing will change between us," Anat said, feeling his need for assurance. "Now tell me your fondest sexual desires."

David was too embarrassed and intimidated to say anything.

"It can't be all that strange, or is it?" she said, with a hint of excitement.

"I'm afraid there isn't much to tell," he said, hoping to put an end to her inquisitiveness.

"Are you being mysterious so you can keep me in a heightened state of curiosity?

"No, that's not it at all."

"Then what is it?"

"I have difficulty... performing," he said, reluctantly.

She looked at him curiously, "Performing for whom?"

"What I mean is ..."

She interrupted. "Is it you can't sustain an erection, or you come too fast?"

"The latter," David admitted after a long pause.

"I find most men like that. Why all the fuss?"

Looking directly at him, she smiled. "Do you know what women love most?"

He was not sure he was ready for what was about to come. "No, but I'm sure I'm about to find out."

"Fingers that can play her like a piano, and a mouth which devours her all over with a delicate, insatiable appetite. Your cock is incidental."

"Well that certainly takes the pressure off, a bit castrating though," David said. "Is that why you prefer women?"

"Women know how to please women. Just like men know how to please men," she said, matter-of-factly.

"Is this to let me know you find men useless, except for your own amusement?"

"On the contrary, I find men an absolute necessity. I need them to appreciate my femininity. I like the way they look at me, the desire in their eyes, their playfulness, and as dancing partners," she admitted.

"Is it only sexually that you prefer women?" he asked, confused.

"No, I like them both. It's just that with women I don't have to pretend. I can be more honest with who I am and what I want. Being an Israeli woman, I need men for my survival."

"What do you mean?"

"On the battlefield, men are far superior to women. I need them to save my life."

The conversation with Anat left him feeling rattled in his manhood. He was neither warrior nor lover. In her world, he was an impotent knight, trusted as a confidante and playmate, but not to be taken seriously as a man.

David spent most of his time reading or wandering through the city, trying to overcome his despair, feeling it was so apparent that surely everyone who saw him could sense it. His ability to hear and retain foreign words gave him a natural gift for languages, and he had managed to pick up enough Hebrew to help make his way around. His attempt to speak the language in his British accent seemed to endear him to everyone, making them want to help him.

The city was beginning to grow on him. He wondered if, perhaps, Gideon was right about Jerusalem being like a beautiful woman—mystical, a wondrous beauty, with enticing aromas, lurking with danger.

Mickey's, owned and run by the Syrian Jew and master of Middle Eastern cooking, became his favorite place to eat. In the two months he had been in Jerusalem, he went there often to soothe both his hunger and his loneliness. He enjoyed Mickey's now familiar greeting, "Shalom, Mr. Churchill," which Anat had assured him was due to his British accent, not his appearance. As soon as he sat down, Mickey served him his customary plate of falafel, hummus and salads. David watched as Mickey brushed the lamb and chicken kebobs with marinade as they turned on the giant rotisserie.

"How is life today, Mr. Churchill?"

"Fine, just fine, thank you."

"Have you been following the news?" Mickey asked.

"Not really, should I?"

"The situation not good."

"What situation?"

"With Egypt, they pushing for war."

Sarah lay naked afloat on the Sea of Galilee. The heat was staggering as she floated toward the bright red sun disappearing into the sea. The trees on the bank bent over her, gently swaying, creating a cool breeze over her body. Motionless, she let the sea carry her away from shore. A faceless man bent over her, kissing her softly on the lips, then his mouth moved all over her. Her body began to quiver, yearning for more. He penetrated her softly, sliding in and out as though she were lined with wet silk. She reached her peak, shaking and trembling violently until she broke into sobs.

Sarah woke from her dream. She knew at once who the man was. Never in her life had she had such a dream. She thought she had gone mad, and had been possessed by demons. Frightened by her own passion, she wept, begging *Hashem* to release her from this torment. She promised herself and God that whenever the Englishman came to see her father, she would avoid leaving her home until she was certain he was gone; neither would she spy from her window to catch a glimpse of him. She, Sarah, the daughter of Reb Eli, would take hold of herself and stop this madness.

David was well versed at hiding his pain under a camouflage of intelligent questions and good conversation, but Reb Eli saw through his veneer and sensed his emotional turmoil. The rebbe listened as he spoke about his time with the Buddhists, whose practice was to end suffering. David admired them, as he did the Sufis and Hindus, and he was surprised to learn that Reb Eli was familiar with their teachings as well. The rebbe asked him if he found any of his spiritual adventures satisfying.

"Not really," David admitted, sadly.

"Is your dissatisfaction what brought you here?"

"In part. I missed Jonathan as well. I was curious to see what his desire to learn Judaism was all about. Frankly, my father avoids Jews. He finds them too tribal. Polo is his religion; my mother's is Harrods."

David acknowledged that he knew little, if anything, about Judaism and that the ways of the orthodox were completely foreign to him. He confided it was Jonathan's idea to give his heritage a try by meeting with the rebbe. He was skeptical about the existence of God and asked how Judaism differed from any of the other religions.

"Believing in God is not essential. It's how you live your life that matters." Reb Eli's answer surprised him. He'd expected something about the marvels of Judaism. Eager to know the rebbe's thoughts about God, he asked, "What do you believe God is?"

"That's a complex matter which requires study and a meditative practice."

"You mean study of the Torah?"

"That is one of the ways."

"From the little I know, the Torah says all kinds of things, some of them not too godly, like stone the adulteresses," David argued.

"I believe a teaching is from God when it promotes compassion and kindness, rather than conformity. Anything that reflects fear and self-righteousness is from man."

"Do you believe a spiritual practice can help?"

"Help what?"

"Loneliness?"

"Loneliness can be a spiritual practice that leads you to your destiny."

Reb Eli's eyes lit with compassion. He saw David's struggle and his longing to know who he was. "Have faith in your destiny. Follow your heart's deepest yearning. It will never let you down."

"That's a lot to think about. Can we continue this conversation?"

"As long as you come, I'll be here."

When Sarah didn't come down to help prepare the evening meal, Dvorah and Esther became concerned. They sent Miriam to see if anything was the matter. Since childhood, Miriam had always been jealous of Sarah. She wished she had been the one blessed with beauty. She was bothered by the attention Sarah was now getting from everyone in the family. Although Sarah was the youngest and had suffered misfortune, Miriam did not see why everyone had to be so protective of her, especially their father. He treated her like she was the most delicate and precious among them. Miriam knew of other women who were barren or had lost their husbands. None of them expected, or were given, such special treatment.

She remembered how Sarah's husband, Yossi, had always looked at her sister with such admiration and devotion, whereas most husbands, after a while, ignored their wives. They performed their conjugal duties, but otherwise were indifferent to them. What bothered Miriam most of all was that, as much as their father and late mother had loved all of their children, she always knew Sarah was their favorite.

When Miriam asked her why she hadn't come down to help with the evening meal, Sarah said she had forgotten the time. Seeing the clock sitting next to the radio, Miriam suspected this was just another way for Sarah to draw attention to herself.

At dinner, Sarah caught her father gazing at her several times. She averted his eyes, fearing he would suspect something was amiss. Miriam got annoyed when Esther offered to take over Sarah's class the next morning, if she needed more rest. Sarah reassured everyone she was fine, she had just gotten a little forgetful. Dvorah and Esther knew that Sarah never forgot anything, and pretended to believe her, as did the rebbe.

Assuring herself she had acted righteously by avoiding any contact with the Englishman, Sarah removed her *sheitel,* untied her hair and pulled on her warm, white fleece nightgown. Jerusalem's nights were chilly during the winter and houses stayed cold, despite the portable gas heaters everyone used. She warmed some milk, as her mother had often done for her when, as a child, she'd had trouble falling asleep. She remembered how tender the comfort of her mother's voice had been when she sang her to sleep, promising her sweet dreams and tomorrows filled with joy and wonder. Finishing her last drop of milk, she sat on her bed looking at the empty glass, then said the evening prayers before going to sleep.

After an hour, she was still awake, exhausted from her struggle to fall asleep. She turned on the bedside lamp, reached for her book on the table, and randomly opened a page in the *Zohar* that read:

"Sarah heard."

She heard this sphere speaking with her husband:
Someone she had never heard before.
"Sarah heard the Opening of the Tent" who was delivering the good news:
"I will return to you when life is due and your wife Sarah will have a son."

A shiver ran through her. Why had this particular passage been presented to her? The irony of the biblical story of her namesake receiving the message she would give birth to a son filled her with an unbearable longing, a longing for love, a longing to have a child of her own. Why had she herself been forsaken? Why couldn't she conceive? Why had God taken her mother away when she needed her most? Why had Yossi died so young? Feeling she was defeated and cast aside by life, the passage was a painful mockery. Sarah fell into despair that so fatigued her she fell asleep.

Walking back from Mickey's, David felt chilled to the bone by the damp night air. He contemplated going home and warming up the bath, when he remembered he had forgotten to turn on the hot water switch. The prospect of sitting in his cold flat with its inadequate gas heater was not welcoming. If only Jerusalem had pubs where he could sit in the warmth, listening to stories told by men who had drunk too much. In reality, with the exception of Gilly's when he was in London, he rarely went to pubs. Now, he longed to sit in a warm pub and soak up the friendly chatter.

At the bottom of Abu Tor there was a stone wall and, beyond

it, the Old City. David stood there looking out, thinking about Reb Eli's advice to follow his heart's deepest yearning—if only he knew what it was—when he remembered the letter he had received earlier from his parents. They "missed him terribly" and wanted to know how he was faring. Did he see much of Jonathan? Were his visits with Reb Eli "productive?" Mostly, they wanted to know why he hadn't written or phoned.

In the distance, the moon hung over King David's Tomb, with an eerie, soft light. He wondered what his namesake had done on such a night, thousands of years ago. Did he spend the night alongside Beersheba, or did he choose a favorite from his harem? What in the still of Jerusalem's winter nights tugged at a king's heart and soul? And what did he do about it?

The high-posted bed was adorned with vibrant red, gold and royal blue silks as several young nymphs brushed Sarah's long hair, gently stroking her arms and legs as she lay naked. Caressing her body with his hands and mouth, the faceless man looked into her eyes, whispering, "My seed is yours to bear." Sarah felt her body quiver with ecstasy when two snakes appeared at the head of the bed-posts. Screaming with fear, she plunged from high above the bed, falling, falling ...

Just before sunrise, Sarah awoke shaken. She was certain she was possessed by a *dybuk* and losing her mind. The dream lingering on, her body ached to be touched. Never had she felt this kind of passion, not even for her husband. Their lovemaking had been of a different kind. It had been tender and contained by a loving respect. Why did this stranger invade her dreams and evoke such sensations in her body? Consumed by her thoughts and desire, Sarah forced herself to get ready to teach her eight o'clock class. She sat at the small table, eating sliced cucumber with *leben* in pita bread. She sipped her tea, then broke into sobs.

In the courtyard, recomposed and walking toward the girl's yeshiva, the meaning of her dream came to her. She awoke to the realization that she could no longer accept a life sentence of emptiness. Had *Hashem* forsaken her, or was it that she had forsaken herself? Was what she felt for the stranger love or carnality? Whatever it was, it was there and she could not deny it; neither could she imagine that she, an infertile widow from Mea Shearim, would ever be of interest to a man like him.

Sarah was troubled by her revelation and had difficulty teaching the day's biblical portion, the story of Naomi. She was relieved when, at noon, her class broke for lunch. Rifka, a shy girl who rarely spoke, accidentally knocked off the *Tanakh* lying on the corner of Sarah's desk as she left to join the others in the school cafeteria. Rifka quickly picked up the holy book, kissed it, and apologetically handed it to Sarah who saw it had fallen open to the story of Tamar.

All through the day, her mind was preoccupied with the *Tanakh's* falling open at the passage about Tamar. When she brought her father his tea, she asked him about something he often said. "There are no accidents, just the Hand of God awakening us."

The rebbe assured her that whenever we are ready to receive knowledge or an awakening, it can come disguised as a mishap or as an apparently random spoken word or passage in a book of wisdom. "That's why we must always be aware of what comes and presents itself to us."

After dinner, her thoughts followed her upstairs, where she sat on her bed staring at the text, reading and re-reading the passage of Tamar. She tried to pray for guidance, but the relentless clamor in her mind had worn her out. She could no longer think or pray. She gave up trying and laid down in hopes of sleep. Then, without any effort, her mind quieted itself and became like an empty vessel. A serene grace embraced her. Her breath began flowing easily and deeply. Sensing the presence of the *shechinah,* she felt cradled in the remembered comfort of her mother's arms. As this quiet power came over her, she knew she had to trust her instincts and follow the guidance of her own *shechinah.*

THREE

Weeks had passed since Sarah had experienced the holy presence. She spent as much time as she could praying and meditating. She woke in the early mornings when it was still dark and lit a candle, imagining its flame to be the light of the universe, a light that would reveal to her what she must do. When her mission became clear, she knew she must muster the courage to follow through with it. There was no other way.

She dismissed her class early, shortly before two o'clock, eager to begin her task. She promised herself not to succumb to fears and doubts, as she hurried to the souk. Like most days when it rained, the souk was almost empty of shoppers. She stopped at the newsstand. She had been there many times to buy a newspaper, never bothering to look at the magazines. Now, she looked carefully through a fashion magazine, searching for photos of modern, young women. She noted how they darkened their eyes and lashes, wore bright lipstick, and dressed in skimpy, short dresses with high heels. She thought they looked foolish. Toward the back of the magazine was a photo of a young model advertising household cleaning products. The model's physique and hair color were similar to hers. She was attractive and wore a simple emerald-green dress with short cap sleeves. Sarah thought the dress lovely and admired how it accentuated the model's slender body. Having never worn a dress without sleeves, she decided she would copy the exact dress, adding long sleeves.

Rushing back to serve her father his tea, she promised

herself she would return to the souk the next day to search for a similar green fabric and some cosmetics. She knew she could not hesitate, or fear would take over and imprison her forever in her silent world of longing.

The next day, after class, Sarah returned to a now crowded souk to buy several yards of fine cloth, a lipstick, and some makeup to accentuate her eyes. Shopping for the material and cosmetics gave her a rush of excitement and strengthened her resolve. She felt certain nothing would hold her back.

In the evening, after the family meal, Sarah went back to her flat. She had been careful not to reveal any change of mood or demeanor to her father and family. Her intention was hers alone, guided and blessed by the *shechinah.* She began patterning the emerald dress on her small Singer sewing machine, a wedding gift from Yossi's mother. Studying the photo of the model, she realized she did not have a pair of modern shoes. The ones in the photo were a sling-back high heel. She wondered how women managed to walk in them, another thing she would have to learn. She was used to the simple low-heeled, closed shoes that orthodox women wore. Tomorrow afternoon, she would search the flea market for a pair of modern ones, since they would be too costly in town. She needed a style that would not be too high-heeled or expose her toes or heels.

At two o'clock on Friday afternoon, the central bus station at the entrance to the city on Jaffa Road was crowded with soldiers trying to catch the last bus home for the Sabbath.

The toilet at the station was dirty and reeked of urine. Inside the cubicle, Sarah removed her *sheitel* and the rest of her drab attire. She changed into the dress she had sewn, and put on her newly purchased, closed, high-heeled shoes. Looking into the small mirror she had brought with her, she brushed her long hair, then carefully applied the eye makeup and lipstick. When all was completed, she put her orthodox belongings into a large brown knapsack and stepped outside.

As she walked past a bus boarding passengers, she noticed her reflection in its window. She was taken aback to see the attractive, modern woman she had become in just twenty minutes. She walked the few blocks toward Agripas Street, confident no one would recognize her.

Madame Aziza loved to sit alone on Friday afternoons, with her radio tuned to Arabic stations, hoping to hear Umm Kulthum. Umm Kulthum was beloved throughout the Arab world. To hear her sing was to be taken out of time and transported to a place where love and yearning ruled supreme. This Friday, as she sipped her Turkish coffee spiced with rose water, she worried about what she was hearing. The airwaves were filled with Gamel Abdel Nasser's threats of war.

Her thoughts drifted back to her childhood in Alexandria. She remembered the sweetness of Friday afternoons, when her grandmother and mother baked and cooked all day for the Sabbath. Her father, Amram Besalel, had been a successful businessman, selling fine cotton cloth across the region. Like his father before him, he had been a pious man, though wary of his position as an observant Jew in a predominantly Muslim country. Their house was grand compared to most of their neighbors. It was a haven for local Jews who, like them, had fled Syria once oppression there had become intolerable. She remembered the ease and tenderness of her youth, then closed her eyes tightly to shut out the memories that followed. The doorbell interrupted her reverie.

Standing before her was a beautiful, young woman with lush auburn hair softly accentuating her porcelain skin. Dressed in a modest green dress that revealed her slender, but well-proportioned body, Madame Aziza assumed the visitor was a *kalah* who was probably looking for Shoshana, the matchmaker who lived downstairs. Over the years, several young *kalahs* had mistakenly come to her flat looking for Shoshana.

"Madame Aziza?" Sarah asked, cautiously, hoping to hide the way her legs were shaking from her first walk in high heels, and her nervousness, "May I come in?"

"Please," she said, ushering the woman in, curious to know what she wanted.

Seated inside the dramatic parlor, Sarah placed her hands on her lap, trying to act at ease. She spoke with candid determination, "I wish to learn everything you know about men."

Madame Aziza looked at her eyes, thinking they resembled a Persian cat's, and asked, "Are you married?"

"No, not anymore." Sarah spoke in a quiet, polite manner, as though this were an interview for employment.

Wondering if, perhaps, Sarah's husband had left her for another woman, she inquired how she had learned about her house.

"From a relative whose identity I must keep anonymous," Sarah said, honestly.

Madame Aziza was bewildered and inquired, "Why did he send you here."

"He didn't. I came on my own." Fearful she would turn her away, Sarah remembered her father's words, "*The best lie is the truth.*"

Sarah told her the story of how, as a young girl, she had learned of her house from this "relative," but not telling her she was Reb Eli's daughter, or that she came from Mea Shearim. "Some nights I would follow this relative to the bus stop bench across the street to watch your beautiful girls dance before men. When I was alone, I would pretend to be one of them."

Intrigued, Madame Aziza asked if she knew what else took place at her home.

Sarah looked directly into her eyes, "Yes. That's why I'm here."

"Then you know I only teach women who work for me."

"Yes."

She quickly took on a business tone. "I take sixty percent of your earnings."

"You can have a hundred percent, but I get to choose whom to be with," Sarah said, calmly with self-assurance.

"Are you Jewish?" Madame Aziza asked.

"Yes."

"A religious man is unable to be with you."

"I know. I have a particular man in mind, who isn't."

"Which one?"

"The Englishman, who, I believe, will return."

Madame Aziza smiled, "I see. I believe he will, too." Filled with curiosity, she asked, "Have you known this Englishman before?"

"In a way, yes. But he doesn't know me," Sarah said, trying to be truthful.

"Will he remember you?" she asked, growing more inquisitive.

"I don't believe so," Sarah said assuringly.

"What if the handsome Englishman does remember you?" She asked, cautiously.

"He will not and it must never be revealed that I asked to be only with him," Sarah replied.

"How can I be sure he will become a steady customer?"

"You will help me make sure he does."

"Good. We have an agreement. We will meet for an hour every afternoon, until you are ready."

Sarah's eyes brightened, "Will two thirty until three thirty be all right, except Fridays?"

"Are you religious?"

"No, I work late on Fridays."

"What do you do?"

"I take care of an elderly gentleman." Sarah replied, carefully.

"I see. What is your name?"

"Tamar."

From the moment she had seen Sarah standing at her door, she thought there was something odd about the large, brown knapsack she carried. It was the common kind of bag housewives used for shopping at the souk. It did not fit with this young woman and her elegant attire. But in today's world, many things didn't make sense, so Madame Aziza dismissed the incongruity. She believed Sarah's story and also felt the Englishman would be back. By putting them together, she would receive one hundred percent of the money. This young woman's motives, or how long she would stay, were of no concern to her. Over the years, so many women had come and gone with untold stories. She had a business to run, nothing else was her concern.

Her heart pounded so hard, Sarah was sure it was visible to everyone she passed as she hurried back to the bus station. In the reeking lavatory, she quickly transformed herself back into a religious woman, carefully placing the modern dress and shoes into her knapsack. She hurried through the streets back to Mea Shearim, in time to serve her father his afternoon tea in the usual manner, except now, she avoided looking into his eyes.

Having eased his resistance, David now found his meetings with Reb Eli more intimate and relaxed. He no longer felt the need to challenge him and looked forward to the rebbe's insights and wisdom, which never ceased to surprise him. Mostly, David appreciated being accepted for who he was. The rebbe met him, not only with kindness, but as an equal.

Today, it was David who listened, as Reb Eli told him that many of the Hasidim in Mea Shearim wanted him to stop being so welcoming to secular men. They were always trying to convert him to their way of thinking. They felt it best for observant Jews to keep to themselves, within the confines of their community. Reb Eli was of the mind that, since everything in the world was holy, he, as a spiritual leader, should embrace all who sought his guidance. David questioned why that should trouble the Hasidim.

"They are afraid," the rebbe replied. "They feel more secure when they isolate themselves. They worry about me letting in outsiders who could jeopardize their ways. The hardest thing for all of us is to let go of our fear. Fear has its place, but when we allow it to rule us, it loses its purpose and becomes a handicap."

David felt honored that Reb Eli would share with him his conflict with the ultra-orthodox. Unlike talking with his father, which always left him feeling less than himself, his conversations with the rebbe were always empowering.

When their meeting ended, he wanted to embrace the rebbe, but quickly decided not to, thinking it would embarrass both of them.

The rebbe smiled as though he could read David's mind. "In our different ways, we are both outsiders."

Promptly at two thirty the next afternoon, Sarah appeared at Madame Aziza's, wearing the same dress, with the knapsack in her hand.

Madame Aziza was struck with compassion when she saw that the girl was wearing what was probably the only dress she owned, yet had refused to accept any money for being with the Englishman. She saw her vulnerability and began to wonder if somewhere, some time ago, the Englishman might have broken her heart. Enthralled by Madame Aziza, Sarah listened intently, memorizing everything this bewitching woman said, observing her every movement and nuance. Madame Aziza spoke of the ways to awaken men's senses, and the importance of creating fantasies that would stimulate even the most troubled of men.

"Men," Madame Aziza said, "perceive women through how they look, feel, smell, move, and sound. They respond to what you're saying from the tone of your voice, which should always be soft and melodious, especially during lovemaking, when it should never be more than a whisper. Conversation should always be focused on him, and you must wait until he initiates it. Make certain he is made to feel that what he says is of great interest to you. Most importantly, remember to keep eye contact at all times, and observe the rhythm of his breath so that you can attune your breath to his. And never, ever allow him to become aware of what you are doing."

Grateful for Madame Aziza's teachings, Sarah said, "I have so much to learn. Thank you for sharing your knowledge with me."

It was at that moment that Madame Aziza decided to teach Tamar everything she had learned so she could become as fine an enchantress as Jerusalem had ever known.

At three thirty, Sarah politely excused herself, allowing enough time to return to the bus station, where she changed her clothes before hurrying back to Mea Shearim, to serve her father his four o'clock tea and help her sisters prepare the evening meal.

Tamar was a mystery to Madame Aziza. She had known many young women during her twenty years in business. Most of them came to her in dire financial need or had been emotionally scarred early in life, usually by men from their own families, who had dishonored them. Tamar was different. She was a contradiction, as much innocent as she was precocious. She had intelligence and possessed a strong sense of who she was and what she wanted. Although it had been only a few days, with just a few hours spent together, Madame Aziza sensed Tamar could be rebellious, and worried that it could become a problem. The girl absorbed everything she was taught with the perfection of an honor student. She had a natural flair for moving her body in a seductive, graceful manner. What intrigued her most was the girl's genuine politeness and nobility; how much she reminded her of herself, long ago.

The train tracks in the heart of Baka were lit by the full moon. The last of the Sabbath candles flickered in the windows of the homes that stood beside the tracks. The night was perfectly still. David ignored the cold seeping through his jacket as he walked arm-in-arm with Anat. Having spent the evening with Gideon, Ronit, Jonathan and Nilli, everything now felt familiar.

In the past few weeks, he had grown very close to her. They had exposed and entrusted themselves to each other. They could reveal everything about themselves, knowing there would be no judgment or shame. Satisfying as this was for him, it did not fulfill his desire for intimacy.

"Is it my imagination, or did Gideon appear distant this evening?" he asked.

"I've noticed a change since his return from the North," Anat said, after reflecting for a moment. "Though Gideon does have a penchant for being distant when it suits him."

"He seemed a bit troubled though, don't you think?"

"I'm not sure. Could be he's been given an important mission."

"Like what?"

"One thing's for sure, we'll never know," Anat said.

"Are things kept that quiet?"

"When it comes to national security, it's an absolute."

Climbing the hill to Abu Tor, though David was intimidated by Anat's beauty and sexuality, he could no longer contain what was troubling him. The idea of going to Madame Aziza's house had been on his mind for days, and he needed to conjure up the courage to discuss it.

"Anat, what would you think if I told you I was considering paying a visit to a whorehouse?" he blurted, hoping for her approval.

She stopped and looked at him, "Seriously?"

"Yes, highly recommended by the rebbe himself," he said, trying to keep the matter light and humorous.

"Good God. What has become of this holy city? David, why would you go to a brothel when there are hundreds of women who would be only too happy to go to bed with you?"

"That's the problem. They would be eager for me to perform. A professional couldn't care less. It might be a good idea to get me over the hump, no pun intended."

"And then what?"

"I'll become an experienced man who won't make a fool of himself every time he looks at a beautiful, naked woman."

"David, do you think it would help if you tried with me?"

she offered.

"That's generous and kind, but somehow I don't view you as being a simple experiment."

"You might be surprised," Anat flashed a seductive smile, which David found intimidating.

"I'm concerned you might get a disease from one of them."

"Not with these ladies, they come with an insurance policy."

"Are they Jews?"

"I don't know. Does it matter?" David asked, bewildered.

"No, it was a stupid question. Will you promise to give me all the details?"

"You are truly shameless."

"My offer remains open."

When you dance for him, everything from your eyes, hair, your fingers, down to your toes, must move with grace, but speak of intrigue. Captivate him with your dance so that he will be unable to resist you. Only when you see the hunger in his eyes will you disrobe, slowly. Then stop, look deeply into his eyes, and, when you see his eagerness, continue to disrobe, ever so slowly."

Madame Aziza guided Sarah's every move until she achieved the nuances of each movement to perfection. "Use your knees to help sway the hips."

In the dining room, a large glass cabinet displayed small glass bottles of scented oils and spices. Madame Aziza held several of them under Sarah's nose, allowing her to experience each separately. She taught her their effects on the senses. Sarah, herself, became intoxicated by them.

When it was time for Sarah to leave, Madame Aziza smiled affectionately at her. "Where do you know this Englishman from?"

Sarah replied, softly, "That's a long story."

Sarah felt her body go weak when Madame Aziza told her the Englishman had been there the night before. She assured Sarah, "I told him all the girls were busy and he should come back tonight." She smiled. "I'm sure you will entice him so he will return many times."

Not wanting to reveal her panic, or appear unprepared, Sarah found herself asking, simply, "What time?"

"Nine o'clock. Should he become anxious, be sure to offer him a little wine, but not too much."

Sarah's underarms and legs were waxed with a sticky honey by an elderly Moroccan woman employed by Madame Aziza. Ripping off the hair was painful, and cold compresses soaked in an elderflower extract were applied to soothe her skin. Afterwards, Madame Aziza presented her with a sheer, gold costume and a jeweled anklet and bracelet to wear for the evening. Lastly, she gave her a small glass dropper-bottle of wintergreen mints to sweeten her breath, and a mixture of lavender and rose geranium oils to bathe in at home.

The evenings were chilly and dark by eight o'clock. Sarah left Mea Shearim cautiously, unnoticed, just as she had done as a child. The scent of the oils she had bathed in followed her as she escaped through the courtyard to Jaffa Road. Panic gripped her. She knew, if she remained paralyzed with fear, she would continue living to the end of her days bound by the orthodoxy of Mea Shearim. David had awoken a force in her that she could not deny. This was her chance to be with the man who evoked a passion she had never known. She was filled with desire to go beyond the comfort of her world, into unchartered waters where she could possibly drown.

The central bus depot was deserted at that hour. With the stench in the toilet far greater in the evening, she quickly removed her *sheitel,* changing into her modern clothes.

Just as she was approaching the House, panic struck again. She could not breathe or move. Perhaps she had been deluding herself, and what she was about to do was nothing more than an act of madness? Sitting on the bench across the street from the House, Sarah felt a chill seep through her wool coat. Looking up into Madame Aziza's parlor, she remembered the first time she had followed Shimon and her brother. How excited and innocent she had been looking through the windows, watching the girls dance before Isaac. She didn't know if she was shivering from the cold or from fear. Her heart pounding, she prayed with all she possessed for the hand of God to guide her. Within minutes, her breath flowed easily. She no longer felt the cold or the pounding of her heart, only the gentle presence of the *shechinah,* embracing and illuminating her.

Madame Aziza greeted her warmly, like a mother happy to see her daughter. She proudly showed her into "the purple room," boasting how it was reserved for important clients. A flowing net of sheer purple and gold chiffon hung from the ceiling, adorning the bed. The delicate perfume of rose geranium from burning candles permeated the air. A large tapestry on the wall depicted an Egyptian palace with beautiful naked women bathing in a natural spring of flowing water as servants watched over them, pouring oils onto their bodies from long-necked, gold-tipped vases.

The erotic décor embarrassed Sarah, but she trusted Madame Aziza knew how to set the stage for enticing men. The costume she had provided accentuated every part of her body. Looking at herself in the mirror, she imagined this was how women in Egyptian harems must have dressed.

Sarah heard melodic Arabic music flow in from the grand room, a cue that it was time to receive guests.

Tonight, on his way over to Madame Aziza's house, David had felt both excitement and revulsion. He reconsidered Anat's offer of going to bed with him and her warning about contracting a disease, but he convinced himself his anxiety was due to his underlying issue and remembered the rebbe's assurance that "Madame Aziza's girls follow the strictest protection, with cleanliness according to Jewish law."

Sitting in the grand room, David recognized from his previous visit the ladies who were now pampering him. Two of Madame's girls danced seductively before him. Another served him tea spiced with honey, and an orange liqueur which immediately made him feel warm and relaxed. He reassured himself his concerns were groundless.

Thinking he would be invited to choose one of these girls, David realized he found none of them appealing. The women were too full-bodied for his taste. He preferred women who were slender, like Anat. The one serving tea was the finer looking of the three. Just when he thought it would be easier to tolerate being with her, Madame Aziza announced she had personally selected her "most enchanting lady" just for him. She beckoned him to follow her down the hall to the purple room.

Seeing the delicate beauty that stood quietly before him, with her eyes penetrating his, he was awestruck. David stood motionless. After a long moment, Sarah reached out her hand to him. As he took her hand in his, he felt a warm quiver through his body. "I'm sorry, I didn't quite..."

"May I take off your jacket?" Sarah asked, so politely that David responded in kind. "Yes, that would be lovely, thank you." He was so taken aback he did not know what to do or say. "I feel a bit awkward...I've never done anything like this...I mean..."

"I know, I understand," Sarah said, comforting him. His candor and vulnerability eased her fears.

"May I take off your shoes?" she offered, gently.

"It's all right. I'll do it." David removed his shoes, then fumbled taking off the rest of his clothes.

When he stood naked before her, Sarah felt her heart pound so hard she was sure he would hear it. She prayed, *Show me the right way to reach his heart.* Her hand reached for his face, tenderly caressing it.

The prospect of being with this goddess terrified him. He felt his body go weak. He heard himself ask for a glass of water.

A carafe of fresh lemon water stood next to a wine decanter. Sarah poured the water into a glass and brought it to his lips.

Watching him slowly sip the water, she became aroused.

She reached for his hand and guided him to lie down on the bed. Remembering how Madame Aziza had taught her to move slowly and seductively, like a cat, she raised her arms, running her hands through her hair as her hips swayed to the soft exotic music, her eyes never leaving his.

Only when she saw the hunger in his eyes did she disrobe. David stared at her naked, slender body, the perfection of her breasts, and the soft roundness of her hips. He observed every part of her as if she were a work of art.

Sarah moved closer to him, he could no longer hold back his excitement. She saw his humiliation and whispered, "I'm so glad I pleased you." She smiled tenderly and handed him a soft cloth soaked with aloe vera to cleanse with, offering him some wine.

"Yes, thank you," he said, hoping it would relieve his embarrassment.

Sarah wrapped herself in the silk robe and brought the wine decanter to the bed. She poured a full glass and served him.

"Will you join me?" David asked.

"Yes, of course."

David handed her his glass, then poured himself another.

Except for a few sips of sweet *Shabbat* wine, Sarah never drank any alcohol. Sensing that if she joined David in drinking wine it would put him at ease and relax her as well, she slowly sipped it.

"I find you extraordinarily beautiful," David confessed. Bewildered why this woman, who possessed such delicate beauty and was well spoken in English, would work in a whorehouse, he asked, "would it be terribly rude to ask where you are from?"

Remembering Madame Aziza's instruction never to divulge anything about herself as that would disrupt the fantasy, Sarah smiled and said, kindly, "I am much more interested in getting to know you."

David feared he had not only embarrassed himself but had trespassed her boundaries. "You are not what I expected or imagined. I feel ..." She kissed his mouth gently, letting him know there was no need for words or explanation. Desiring to hold and feel her close to him, David reached out and drew her nearer. He stroked her hair and body, desiring to know this woman and give her pleasure.

The tenderness of his touch and the closeness of his naked body deepened the intoxication of the wine. All of Sarah's fears and tension anticipating this moment disappeared. She felt a welcoming, like she was coming home to a place her body and soul remembered from long ago. The spell of that memory entranced her. Before she knew it, she had drifted into sleep.

Enchanted by this lovely woman who had passed out from the wine, David studied every part of her, down to the way she wiggled her toes as she slept so innocently in his arms. How comforting it was to watch her sleep, to enjoy the beauty of her face and body, the smell of her skin and hair against him, how every part of her pleased him.

Sarah awoke, startled. "I'm so sorry, I'm not used to drinking wine."

"I see that," David said playfully.

"I'll be sure to tell Madame Aziza, so she won't charge you."

"It's all right. When you fell asleep, I went out and paid her for the entire evening. You can sleep as long as you like."

"You needn't have done that, I'm so—"

"Don't be," he interrupted.

She reached for his hand, touching and marveling at each of his fingers.

David felt the invitation for tenderness. The face he had been studying now seemed so familiar. He began to slowly caress her.

Sarah felt her entire being succumb to him. She lay quietly, allowing him to discover her on his own terms.

Seeing the desire in her eyes, her body warm with passion, breathing harmoniously with him, David desired only to please her and was able to hold himself.

She welcomed him inside her. Her loneliness and sheltered life diminished with each slow, deliberate move of his body rhythmically pressing against hers as his mouth and hands slowly, tenderly gave her pleasure. Her body reeled with spasms of joy as she reached her peak.

David surrendered to her, entering a world he never knew existed, oneness with a woman who brought forth all his passion and desire.

Sarah woke just before sunrise. She quietly dressed, grabbed her bag, which she had hidden under the bed, and left David deep in sleep.

The stairway was completely dark. At the bottom was a narrow space behind the stairs. She knew there was not enough time to go to the bus depot, change, and be home before the men went to prayer. The area had a low ceiling, barely allowing her to stand as she quickly changed back into her orthodox garb. She tied up her hair and blindly searched through the bag for her *sheitel,* clumsily covering her head with it.

The streets were still dark as she rushed home to Mea Shearim, where the morning prayers would soon begin. Like a thief scurrying for her life, she made sure she was not seen.

By seven o'clock, the sun was coming through her bedroom window. She bathed, dressed, ate her pita bread with slices of cucumber mixed in *leben,* and hurried to teach her eight o'clock biblical class.

In the parlor, the sun was shining through the windows, throwing brilliant beacons of light. Madame Aziza lay leisurely on the sofa, sipping Turkish coffee.

David, dazed from sleep, came in. "Good morning."

"Good morning. Would you like a cup of tea?" she asked, cheerfully.

"No, thank you," David said, shyly.

Madame Aziza inquired if the evening had gone well.

He assured her "it went very well," and matter-of-factly asked the name of "the lady."

She was pleased and told him her name was Tamar. She continued about what a beautiful day it was, in the genteel manner of a proprietress running an English bed and breakfast where he was a guest.

Trying not to show how urgent or excited he was to see Tamar again, David casually inquired, "Is she available this evening?"

Madame Aziza told him he would have to call later, as Tamar only worked part time and did not have a telephone. She had to rely on her calling in to know her availability.

Continuing in a casual manner, he asked if Tamar lived nearby. She told him, in the kindest terms, "out of respect for all my girls' privacy, I never divulge any information about them."

"I understand."

It took all of Sarah's strength to concentrate on the day's lesson and continue teaching her class. Absorbed with thoughts of David, she replayed their night together over and over, each time becoming more aroused by her memories. When the *bat mitzvah* girls demanded more of her insight into the story of Ruth, she urged them to go deeper into their own minds, and seek the answers for themselves.

Euphoric and exhausted, she was overcome with a great sense of relief when her class ended. Having had little sleep the night before, she went home and collapsed on her bed. She slept through the afternoon and awoke to her sister, Miriam, knocking on the door to inquire if she was all right. She told her she hadn't slept well the night before and apologized for having slept through their father's afternoon tea.

"Father was concerned you weren't feeling well," Miriam said.

Sarah offered to dress quickly and run down to join their father for afternoon tea. Miriam assured her there was no need. She could continue to rest, "Father is busy talking to the Englishman."

The dramatic change in David astounded Reb Eli. In all his years of seeing young men visit Madame Aziza for help, he had never witnessed such an immediate and profound transformation. David's buoyancy and optimism filled the room.

David had called earlier, begging to see him. The rebbe heard the urgency in his voice and invited him to tea. By the manner in which he repeatedly thanked him for guiding him to Madame Aziza, one would think an arranged marriage had been happily consummated. Although feeling concerned, the rebbe was careful not to diminish David's high spirits. Instead, he told him how happy he was that Madame Aziza had helped him find a way to overcome his inhibitions. Now that David felt confidence in his body, the rebbe wished him "blessings and much *mazel* to go out and find your *beshert.*"

"Beh . . . shert?"

"Your soulmate."

After their visit, Reb Eli read the letter he had received from David's father. Phillip was grateful to him for taking his son under his wing. He pleaded with him, as he had so many times before, to let him know if there was anything the rebbe needed. He asked Reb Eli if he would be kind enough, when time allowed, to drop him a note on David's progress, mentioning that his son was not in the habit of writing. Lastly, he inquired, "How is your bereaved daughter, Sarah, faring?"

His senses heightened to every sight and smell, David walked through the city seeing everything as if for the first time. He noticed the brilliance of the light, how the sun illumined every stone in Jerusalem. He could even feel the heat from the stone pavement penetrate the soles of his shoes, spreading up and warming his body. Feeling vibrant and alive, he felt a pang of hunger and decided to go to Mickey's.

"Shalom, Mr. Churchill," Mickey greeted him, brightly.

"Shalom Mickey." David sat down at his customary table next to the counter and ordered a large plate of all the mixed salads. He ate hungrily, thanking Mickey for the perfection of his food.

Whenever David came in to eat, which he often did, Mickey thought of him as a quiet loner. Today, Mickey sensed a warmth and exuberance he had not seen before, and said, "Looks like life is treating you good, eh?"

"Not bad Mickey, not bad."

"Did you find a *kalah?*"

"A kal-ah?" David asked.

"A woman to be your wife."

"Not exactly, Mickey."

Consumed with his thoughts of Tamar, David telephoned Madame Aziza from the booth at the corner of Mickey's street. Delighted when she answered immediately, he asked if Tamar was available for the evening. She informed him she had not yet heard from her and promised to call him the minute she did. Unable to hide his frustration and eagerness, he asked if she would please be so kind as to book all of the girl's available evenings for the rest of the month.

His conversation with Madame Aziza left him lonely and troubled. Although he had just eaten, there was a hunger in the pit of his stomach. He called Anat, hoping she could meet him at Café Cassis. There was no answer. David's longing to be with Tamar intensified, even as he fretted about getting so carried away by a woman who was, after all, a prostitute.

Madame Aziza had learned long ago to listen carefully and trust her intuition. The moment Tamar had told her she could keep all the money, she knew there was a great deal at stake for the girl. She ruminated, why this Englishman? Yes, he was young and handsome, but how did Tamar know about him? Had she previously been with him and, if so, why had he not remembered a girl like her? She was puzzled about what role the Englishman had played in Tamar's life. Her curiosity grew whenever she thought about the girl.

Each time she had tried to find out more about her, Tamar had become more secretive. Whenever she looked into her beautiful, beguiling face, she became more intrigued. There was something in it that reminded her of a time in her own life, so long ago. With just a few hours before her clients arrived, Madame Aziza sat gazing out to the street where, in the far distance, the sun was sinking behind the hills of Jerusalem as her thoughts wandered to Egypt.

Jamila Grazi had been a beautiful young woman, living in Alexandria, wanting nothing more than to please her husband, Micah, a prominent businessman whose family owned real estate in the city. He was handsome, adoring and well educated. Jamila loved and admired him. Her ambition in life was to please him and give him the many sons he desired. But when she did not conceive after four years of marriage, Micah divorced her and immediately remarried her lifelong friend, Jasmine. She was devastated.

The entire congregation at the Zaradel Synagogue, where Jamila's family belonged and where she had been married, knew about her plight, adding to her humiliation. Her parents had come to Egypt from Syria, where most of their family still remained. Her father owned one of the fine fabric shops in the Jewish quarter and Jamila had enjoyed a comfortable life, never having to work. She had been groomed to be a good wife, mother and respected member of her community.

After her husband divorced her, Jamila had no alternative but to return to her parents' household. She lived there until they died in nineteen forty-eight, the same year the new State of Israel was born. Jamila, an only child, was left alone in the world, at twenty-five.

Madame Aziza remembered. She remembered her life when she was still the young Jamila Grazi, a Jewess living alone at a time when it seemed the whole of Egypt came to suspect that every Jew was a Zionist spy. She remembered how, as a young girl, she had always been fond of the "gypsy woman" who lived nearby, down by the port, and who came frequently to purchase the finest cloths from her father's shop. She had a contagious smile and, whenever she passed by, a wave of fine-scented oils lingered in the air after her.

Soon after her parents died, Jamila took over her father's shop. The gypsy woman befriended her. She confided to Jamila that those close to her knew her as "Madame Aziza." Taking a strong interest in Jamila, she invited her to her home, where she consoled her wounded spirit. It was there that Jamila was awakened to the alluring power of the feminine.

Jamila Grazi learned that being a woman meant more than bearing children, or being subservient to a man. Madame Aziza taught her how to honor the gifts of her body and spirit, how to give pleasure to herself as well as a man, and how to trust in her feminine instinct and intuition. She introduced her to the secrets of exotic oils and herbs—how to apply them to the erogenous zones and enhance the pleasures of the senses—and the importance of dressing in costumes that please the eye, as well as the art of dance, where every part of the body moves easily, rhythmically, with the hypnotic seduction of a snake, while the eyes penetrate another's soul, the hands touching gently with attentiveness to every delight of the body—all as a gateway to the temple of the soul, the source of all that blesses and praises goodness and pleasure.

Jamila Grazi learned well. Wealthy men began to swarm around her like bees to honey. She chose only those who pleased her and adorned her with gifts. When they no longer suited her, she simply dropped them. Having been groomed and treated as a daughter, Jamila, in turn, looked after Madame Aziza and her affluent business, one of Alexandria's best-kept secrets.

Jamila's life became gilded, with well-to-do suitors requesting her hand in marriage. Just when she thought she had everything, Nasser came to power. He ordered all Jews to leave the country immediately. After two thousand years in Egypt, he allowed them to take one suitcase each. "No Return" was stamped in their passports.

Madame Aziza remembered her namesake with fond memories, grateful for the gifts she had received. They had enabled her to flourish and never want for anything. Except to have a child of her own.

When Madame Aziza had asked Tamar to be certain she took precautions not to become pregnant, something she required of all the girls who worked for her, Tamar assured her she needn't worry, as she was unable to conceive. She knew this young woman, who occupied her mind, was very much like herself and, therefore, she could be certain Tamar would never reveal who she really was.

FOUR

Ever since the night with David, Sarah could think of nothing but being with him again. It took all of her energy and concentration to teach her class and behave normally around her family. She telephoned Madame Aziza, hoping to hear if she had heard from David. When she heard "the Englishman called. He wants to book every evening you are available this month," she felt exhilarated and could not contain her excitement. Only after she hung up did fear set in about how she would continue managing to steal away to Madame Aziza's. How long would it be before someone noticed she was gone at night, or discover what she had done? Her head spun with terror-filled thoughts of what could happen, as she became queasy with panic.

She had told Madame Aziza she needed to arrange for someone to look after the elderly gentlemen she worked for, and that she would call to let her know which nights she was available. The one thing Sarah knew for certain was that she would find a way to continue being with David.

David was obsessed with Tamar. He waited all day near the telephone, afraid to go out in case he missed a call from Madame Aziza. He did not want to appear desperate and keep calling to ask if she had heard from her. The phones in Israel were temperamental. At times, they didn't work for hours, sometimes even for days, adding to his frustration. The weather had turned warm, and he lay out on the roof reading and basking in the sun as the city shifted from dawn to dusk through a vivid kaleidoscope of pink, amber, blue and violet light.

The phone rang and David felt a rush of excitement. It was Jonathan asking why he hadn't heard from him. David told him he had been preoccupied with the rebbe and would catch up with him soon. After hanging up, he felt ashamed for not telling the truth. He needed to share his dilemma with someone he could trust to be nonjudgmental and understanding. He called Anat, asking if she would join him for wine, and "anything else that is in the fridge."

Anat had spent the day at an archeological dig on the outskirts of Jerusalem, not far from a *moshav* called Beit Zeit. She was, as usual, "starving." David emptied his refrigerator of its contents—a small piece of cheese, yogurt, jam, crackers, and stale pita bread. Anat devoured everything within minutes.

"You would never make a proper English lady."

"I should hope not," Anat mimicked, in a perfectly posh British accent.

He poured two hefty glasses of wine while she ate the remaining cheese, spreading jam on it. He delighted in her insatiable appetite and wondered whether it would make her fat and matronly as she grew older. He took a long sip of his wine and told her he had visited Madame Aziza's bordello.

"How fantastic! I want to hear every detail. What did they look like, what did they do … everything?"

David laughed, "You're incorrigible."

"Of course. Why else would you want to be with me?"

"Actually, there's not much to tell, just that it was a lovely experience."

"Lovely? You spend an evening with a whore and all you can

say about it is that it was 'lovely'?" Anat was not amused by the lack of detail and drama she had hoped for.

"She was amazingly beautiful, gentle and kind. Her name is Tamar," David said, sorry to have disappointed Anat.

"What? She sounds like the ones in Hollywood movies. They are always beautiful, kind-hearted and tragic."

"Had I known, I would have gone to the cinema more often."

"Seriously David, what did this Tamar do to make you feel this way?"

"I can't quite explain it without sounding ridiculous."

She looked at him, waiting to understand and hear more.

"She made me feel so alive!"

"How did she do that? Was it the way she fondled you or…"?

"Actually, she did none of that. It was more the way she moved, smelled, felt, the gentleness of her voice and touch. When I embarrassed myself in the usual way, she made nothing of it, and I simply forgot I had a problem. I became totally engrossed in everything about her, not me. That's what made it so marvelous."

"I don't understand."

"I'm not sure I do either. That's why I have to see her again." David confessed.

Anat was disappointed by the lack of erotic details.

"I'm happy one of Madame Aziza's girls made you feel good about yourself. Be careful not to get too carried away."

David woke early and decided he would go down to the corner grocer to pick up the *Jerusalem Post* and some fresh pita bread. He barely reached the bottom of the stairway when he heard his telephone ring. Climbing three steps at a time, he rushed through the door, lunging for the phone. He tried to withhold his excitement when he heard Madame Aziza. Her voice was cheerful with enthusiasm announcing, "Tamar is available this evening."

His heart racing with anticipation for the night to come, he ran down to the street. He wished passers-by a cheery "good morning." But by the time he got back to the flat, he was troubled. Why was he so excited and worked up over a prostitute? Why had he committed to paying for all her available evenings for a month? Where was his "good judgment," as his father would ask?

Sarah made certain to be as punctual and present as ever for her family duties. She behaved as she always had, in order to avoid bringing any attention to herself. Still, she was cautious around her father, avoiding direct eye contact, for fear the slightest nuance would alert him to the change in her. At dinner, her four-year-old niece, Malkia, asked if she would braid her hair and sing her favorite songs. It had been some time since Sarah had braided the little girl's hair and sung to her. She wondered how she had sensed the change in her. Malkia told her she was glad she was feeling better and didn't have children of her own because it meant she had more time to play with her. Sarah responded good-naturedly, telling Malkia if she had children of her own, she would have more cousins to play with. The little girl said, simply, "I already have enough."

Dvorah laughed at Malkia's remark. She was glad to see Sarah engage with Malkia and the children. Not since Yossi had died had Sarah, who adored the children, shown any interest in them. Perhaps, she thought, Sarah's mourning period was over and, in time, she would find a new husband.

Lately, Reb Eli had been noticing the change in his daughter. She seemed to have finally adjusted to her circumstances and displayed more of her old cheerful disposition. Yet something didn't seem quite right. There was a shroud of distance about her, which was not like Sarah. He wondered why she avoided looking at him. In any event, watching her play with the children, as she had always done before the death of her husband, warmed his heart. Perhaps a young woman, unable to have children of her own, who lost a husband at a young age, was, after all, able to find peace. The rebbe felt grateful for seeing the return of her cheerfulness and thanked *Hashem* for the blessing.

She had less than an hour to get ready. Sarah gathered the modern things she had hidden in her linen closet, carefully placing them in her knapsack. The courtyard was dark and quiet, with just the sound of a baby crying. Most of Mea Shearim at this hour was busy with evening prayers. She hurried through the courtyard, down the narrow street, until she was safely out of sight.

The Purple Suite was once again reserved for her. A large bouquet of fresh, white lilies stood dramatically in a copper and gold oriental vase on the dresser. A sheer white cotton nightgown lay on the bed for her to slip into. The gown revealed the outline of her body with delicate enticement, inviting the eye to search for more.

Madame Aziza was pleased when she came in to see Tamar

and, in her motherly manner, brushed her hair, reminding her to remain poised and confident with the Englishman. "Remember, men are warriors. They like feeling they have power over you. Stay quietly aware of his needs. Allow him to think you need to be conquered, so he will desire and want you more." Madame Aziza asked if her body was "fresh and fragranced with the proper oils for the Englishman to smell and taste." Sarah assured her she was ready to receive him.

During her final preparations, Sarah remembered all of the many things she had learned from Madame Aziza: the subtle ways men enjoyed being seduced; how the eyes alone should speak; how the lips should hold a sensuous, mysterious smile; the secrets of the erogenous areas of their bodies; how and when to stimulate spellbinding orgasms; to remember men's feminine side, which desired to be made love to like a woman; and, above all, never to let them know what you are thinking or what you are going to do next. There was so much to learn. How sheltered and naïve she had been, knowing nothing at all about men. She just assumed they were all like Yossi, simple, gentle, with no expectations. What most astounded her was how little she knew about herself.

David checked his watch for the third time. In fifteen minutes he would be with Tamar. Suddenly, it occurred to him, what if she has already been with a client? After all, she did this for money, and Madame Aziza could have booked her earlier with someone else. His agreement with Madame Aziza was to book Tamar for all her available nights. That didn't mean she could not book her beforehand with someone else.

His thoughts troubled him and made him feel ill. He tried to assuage his fears and reassured himself that he had made it clear to Madame Aziza to book Tamar for the entire night. Tonight, he told himself, would be his last visit. He needed to accept the reality of who Tamar really was. Now that he had learned to overcome his problem, he was confident he could find intimacy with a woman other than a prostitute.

Seeing Sarah standing beside the white lilies in her white gown, he was struck by how angelic, yet magnificently sensual she looked. The sight made him want to sweep her up in his arms. Instead he caught hold of himself and simply said, "Hello." He was certain he saw her blush.

She poured him a glass of wine and held it to his lips. Not wanting to become intoxicated and fall asleep, she asked, "Would it be all right if I just take a sip of yours?"

"Of course," he said, offering her his glass.

Taking a sip from David's glass, Sarah remembered her wedding, the ritual of drinking from the same cup and, for a brief second, imagined they, too, were standing under the marriage *chupah.*

The music this evening was different. It was soft and melodic, which David found soothing. This time, there was no dancing, just her eyes searching his.

Eager to be with her, he lay down on the bed waiting.

Sarah reached for a small blue bottle of lavender oil on the bedside table. She poured some into her hands, then began messaging his chest. The calming scent filled his nostrils. Remembering Madame Aziza's words, "your touch holds everything you feel and desire," her hands began to caress his shoulders, moving slowly down his arms, hands and fingertips, kissing each of his fingers. Her hands moved down to his inner thighs and muscular calves. She massaged his feet, giving his toes the same attention as his fingers. The touch of her gentle hands aroused and delighted him. He turned to her, saying, "Now it's my turn." She undressed slowly, allowing him the pleasure of seeing her body.

Anat's words echoed in David's head, "It's what the hands and mouth do that interest women the most." With that in mind, he gently massaged Sarah's body. Caressing her breasts, he gently stimulated her erotic zones. The smell of her body enticed him. His mouth swept over her and into every crevice. Sarah moaned with delight and her pleasure empowered him. Their bodies, oiled in lavender, glided together in a harmonious rhythm, reaching the delirious culmination of their lovemaking. Afterward, lying in his arms, she turned from him so he could not see her weeping silently into the feathered pillows.

She thought of Yossi, remembering how his hands had felt soft and gentle, like a child's. His mouth had suckled her like an eager infant. Shame and remorse swelled within her. She prayed for God's forgiveness, for judging and comparing her dead husband's lovemaking to David's.

Before sunrise, Sarah slipped out of bed to leave. David awoke, "It's so early. Where are you going?"

"Home."

"Let me take you there."

"No, that's not possible."

"Why?"

"Please don't ask questions," she pleaded.

"Who are you?"

"I'm who you see."

"When can I see you again?"

She wanted so much to say tomorrow and every day after that, but simply answered, "Next Sunday."

"You need the money, why not see each other sooner and more often," David offered.

His words cut into her heart. "It's too difficult," she whispered.

"Then I'll wait till Sunday."

Fearful that he would try to follow her, she left Madame Aziza's house watching over her shoulder every step of the way until she safely reached the bus depot. Changing her clothes inside the lavatory, she wept. Just hours before, her body knew joy. Now, it knew the bitter pain that the man she loved with all her heart thought she was nothing more than a competent whore whose services he desired. She told herself this was the end of her charade, promising to end it.

On the Mount of the Hebrew University, David lay on the grass, basking in the warmth of the sun, waiting for Jonathan to arrive. The day was warm, with the promise of spring budding everywhere. The air was clear and the sweet smells of blossoms permeated the Mount. Feeling alive and vibrant as never before, he imagined what it would be like to have Tamar laying there beside him.

Jonathan arrived twenty minutes late, which was unlike

him. He apologized for being tardy, saying he had been at a conference about the rising tension along the country's borders. Nasser's constant rhetoric was taking its toll. "Everyone fears war is imminent."

"War?"

"Yes."

"That's preposterous."

"Why is it preposterous?"

"What on earth do the Arabs want? There's no oil here, or anything else worth fighting over."

"They want Israel gone."

"Why?"

"God knows."

"Surely this strip of land can't mean that much to them," David said, trying to understand.

"Unfortunately it does. Well, there's nothing we can do about it. Let's hope, by some miracle, it all works out," Jonathan said, hoping to dismiss the tension he was feeling. "How are things going with the rebbe?"

"Very well. We've become quite chummy," David said, with a sense of pride.

"I spoke with your mum and dad. They wanted to know how you were doing, why you haven't called or written. I told them you were contemplating becoming an orthodox Jew."

"Splendid. What a fright. That's my mother's worst nightmare. How would she explain to her tea party chums that her one and only son had gone native in Israel?" David took a deep breath, his prelude to raising a difficult or awkward subject. "Lovely day isn't it?"

"Yes, looks like winter is behind us. I'm quite looking forward to the summer. Should you decide to stay on longer, we can go to the sea," Jonathan promised.

"Actually, I might like that," David said, anticipating what he was about to reveal.

"Good. Rebbe's caught your attention, has he?"

"Actually, a certain lady has."

"Super. When can we meet her?" Jonathan exclaimed, delighted with David's news.

"You can't."

Jonathan looked bewildered, "Why not?"

David took another deep breath, "She's a prostitute."

Jonathan laughed. "Very funny."

"I'm not joking."

Jonathan looked at David to see if he was being serious. When he saw the sadness in his eyes, he knew it was true. "Have you gone mad?"

"She's the most beautiful, incredible woman I've ever met. She makes me feel like I've never felt before, or probably ever will."

"For God's sake, David, that's what she's paid to do."

"I know ... but somehow I believe she really desires me, that it's sincere. It's in her eyes, the way she touches me, makes love to me. It feels so genuine and alive."

"This is beginning to sound like the time you convinced me you knew how to drive the Land Rover," Jonathan said, hoping to bring David back to reality.

"I was fifteen then."

Jonathan tried to hold back his fear and anger. "What makes

you think your judgment is any better now?"

"Hopefully, I've matured a bit."

"Good God, David, this is awful. You've got to get hold of yourself. You don't fall in love with a bloody whore. That's sheer madness."

"Then I've gone mad. I can't keep her out of my mind. She occupies my every thought," David confessed.

"This is as bad as the threat of war. Perhaps it's best you return home until all this blows over."

"I think you're becoming a bit hysterical."

"Has she helped you overcome your difficulty? Is that it?" Jonathan asked, trying to keep his composure.

"It's much more than that."

"With all of the women here, choosing to fall for a prostitute is sheer insanity. Surely you can find someone who is sincere and worthy of your affection."

David knew it was hopeless trying to explain his feelings for Tamar, when he himself was struggling with them. He stood quietly, hoping Jonathan would relent.

"You've got to stop this before it turns into something dreadfully embarrassing. You must promise not to see her again, ever. Just cut it off," Jonathan said, half pleading, knowing nothing would stop David once he was set on something.

"What if that's not possible?"

"Anything is possible. This is no time to be frivolous, David!"

"I'm sorry this troubles you. It does me as well."

Sarah had been looking forward to the Passover celebration. It was a time to remember and honor the struggle of her ancestors and the joy of their journey to the Promised Land. She saw it as an opportunity to escape from the despair of living in the desert of her own self into a land of peace and hope. With just a week to go, she would be busy with all the preparations.

During dinner, her father announced he had invited David to their Passover *seder.* Sarah fell into a panic. She felt her heart pounding and feared everyone could hear it. She left dinner as soon as she could, and lay awake thinking what to do. Since she hadn't been able to sleep, she was unable to function at work. She caught her students looking at her suspiciously, wondering what was wrong with their teacher. She was barely able to concentrate on the teaching of Passover, or anything else. She was consumed with finding a way out of attending the *seder.* The only thing that came to mind was feigning illness. The idea worried her as it would also bring unwanted attention. In her desperation, she even imagined checking herself into the hospital for severe stomach pain, but feared it would bring back painful memories for her father. She remembered how many times her ailing mother had had to be taken to the hospital. She knew this ploy would only bring suffering to her father, something she found unbearable. That night, not knowing what to do, she lay awake, praying for a way out, when she remembered her father's offer to send her abroad. Feeling that would be the best solution, she decided to tell the rebbe she would like to accept his offer, and, since the school would be closed for Passover, she thought then would be a good time to go.

Plagued and exhausted by her thoughts, Sarah helped her sisters prepare the kitchen for Passover. They discarded all the *humitz,* the leavened grains that are forbidden during the seven days of the holiday. All four sisters carefully scrubbed the cupboards, dishes, pots and utensils, making sure everything was clean and renewed.

The rebbe had spent most of the day at the synagogue. Now, he was busy in his study, counseling a visitor. As soon as the session was over, she would tell him of her decision to go to New York, where her mother's uncle lived in Borough Park, among the other Hasidim. Surely he would understand? But what if he insisted Passover was not the time to leave, and asked her to wait until after the holiday? Would this leave her with no option but to show up for the *seder*? Tortured with anxiety, she wondered if it was a mistake to even ask her father. Perhaps it would be best to go back to the option of feigning illness? She was scrubbing the kitchen floor when the rebbe came in asking for his tea and announcing, casually, "The young man from England will be unable to join us for the *seder.*"

Feeling a huge surge of relief, Sarah thanked God for resolving her predicament. Her exploit would not be discovered. She would not have to fake being ill or escape to a foreign land during *Pesach.* After days of anguish, she collapsed into a deep sleep, sleeping soundly for the first time since hearing David had been invited to their *seder.*

Jonathan had insisted David join him with Nilli, Ronit and Gideon for Passover at Kibbutz Gadot, where Gideon and Nilli's parent's lived. He said it would give him an opportunity to see the northern part of the country, especially the ancient Galilean city of Safed and the Sea of Galilee.

Jonathan warned him he would be bored at the rebbe's *seder* as it would be a long and tedious religious affair. He had offered to let the rebbe know that David was joining him at Kibbutz Gadot's *seder*. David suspected Jonathan had orchestrated this Passover plot to get him out of the city and away from Tamar.

He felt like the odd man out on the trip up to the Galilee. He was sorry that Anat, who was also invited, had decided to spend the Passover with her parents in Jerusalem. Her brother, Ilan, had been called up to do army duty, *milluim*, something all Israelis under fifty-four were obliged to do each year. She had told him she couldn't, in good conscience, leave her parents alone for the holiday. He missed having her with them and realized how much he relied on her as a confidant.

After five hours on winding, dusty roads in Gideon's cramped Volkswagen, driving through Metula and Rosh Pina, they began the climb up the mountain to Safed. They were all weary from the drive. Nilli, Gideon and Ronit sang children's songs. Jonathan and David attempted to follow. Their British accent in Hebrew made everyone laugh. Ronit tried to teach them how to pronounce the guttural sounds. Attempting to do so made their accents even more comical. Everyone began mimicking each other, laughing at their own absurdity. David remembered how good it was to feel like a child again.

At thirty-two hundred feet in the Upper Galilee, Safed commanded magnificent views of the mountainous region, with its ranges of hills and high peaks, its streams and lakes, and its dense groves of trees. Gideon pointed out Mount Hermon's snow-capped peak, straddling the border between Israel, Syria and Lebanon, and Mt. Meron to the west. The Amud Valley was below them. To the east stood the Golan Heights, and, to the south, lay Tiberias and the Sea of Galilee. David felt exhilarated by its beauty. He had the strange feeling he had been there before and was glad to have returned.

Gideon suggested they come back in early June for a hike down the Amud Valley, when it would be full of butterflies and the wildflowers would be in full bloom. "We can cool off in the springs of Ein Koves and at the Ein Seter waterfall." David said he loved hiking and would like to stay on to join them. Jonathan knew why he really wanted to stay.

Nilli and Ronit had made plans to visit their friend, an artist from the Hebrew University who now lived in Safed. They arranged to meet up with the men later.

Wandering through the winding alleyways of Safed, between houses of ancient stone shaded by arbors of grapevines, David felt like he was moving through a painting by an Old Master. Gideon pointed out the medieval synagogues and told how the Jews who had been expelled from Spain and Portugal had settled there and developed the town. David was impressed by his intimate knowledge of the city and wanted to learn more. They went to Gideon's favorite restaurant, Bagdad Café, where they were to meet up with Nilli and Ronit.

The café was inviting, with outdoor tables overlooking the valley. The weather was perfect. David was smitten by the antiquity of the place, and wanted to know more of its history. Gideon warmed to his interest and told him how, in the sixteenth century, many Jewish scholars and mystics had moved there, fleeing the Inquisition that followed the Spanish

Expulsion. Being one of the four holy cities of Judaism, along with Jerusalem, Hebron and Tiberias, Safed became the spiritual center where kabbalists such as Rabbis Yitzhak Luria and Shlomo Alkabetz established the city's standing as a kabbalist haven.

A pigeon's dropping fell directly on David, spattering his forehead. Gideon laughed, saying his mother believed "when a bird poops on you, it is a sign of good luck."

"I wouldn't bank on it," David said as he went to wash it off.

Coffee and chocolate cakes were brought out as he returned. Gideon was telling Jonathan about all the years of suffering that had taken place in Safed, due to earthquakes, plagues and later, the ongoing Arab attacks. Gideon proudly told them of the liberation of Safed during the War of Independence.

"In 1948, the Jews here were mostly elderly, young children and orthodox scholars. So when the fighting began, they were outnumbered more than ten to one by heavily-armed Arabs. They were desperate. They had an old artillery piece that didn't do much more than make noise. They fired it anyway, hoping the explosion would frighten the Arabs away. Then a miracle happened. It started raining. It never rains here in May. The way the elders tell it, the old ladies of the town were accustomed to calling out to each other, the Jews in Arabic, and the Arabs in Yiddish.

"When they heard the cannon, the Arab women called, "*Vos is dos?*" to which one woman replied, "We have the bomb." The Jewish soldiers then started a rumor that "everyone knows it always rains after an atomic blast." The Arabs were convinced the Jews had used the atom bomb, and that the rain was radioactive fallout. So, in the midst of a battle in which they had the upper hand, they fled the city in panic. And that's how, in May, 1948, the battle of Safed was won."

David wondered how much truth was in this story. It seemed the Jews had so many claims to miracles. Intrigued by Safed, he said, "I'd like to spend more time here."

Gideon smiled, "Good. Safed, to be truly appreciated, requires time alone, like being with a beautiful woman whose real charm lies hidden, available only to those who deserve her attention."

"Why do you compare cities like Jerusalem and Safed to women?"

"Because they, too, are mysterious and holy."

Jonathan felt obliged to add a Judaic note to Gideon's reply. "That's what's known as the *shechinah,* the feminine aspect of God's presence, which the mystics say rests above Safed."

They stopped for a late lunch by the shore of Lake Kinneret, ordering a fish called "bouri" that resembled trout and came marinated in fresh garlic, lemon, olive oil and parsley. David thought it the best fish he had ever tasted and well worth the trip. Gideon pointed out "where Jesus was rumored to have walked on water." He asked David if he would like to attempt the same feat. There were four witnesses; should he succeed, all would know he was the new messiah. David politely declined, saying the ambiance, fish and company were more than enough entertainment for one afternoon. Besides, having a stomach full of food, he would sink like a stone and embarrass himself.

By the time they reached the Upper Galilee, David was

enthralled. Other than Jerusalem, he hadn't seen much of the country. Jonathan was right. This trip had introduced him to a wider view of Israel. Most importantly, it allowed for his timely return to Jerusalem and his Sunday rendezvous with Tamar.

They arrived at the kibbutz in time for the Passover *seder* and were greeted enthusiastically by Nilli and Gideon's parents, Leon and Rifka Hurvitz. The Hurvitzes were sincere, open-hearted people who clearly exalted their children. Their love for them shone for all to see. David couldn't help feeling envious. He had never felt anything like that from his own parents. The Hurvitzes were pleased to see Ronit and Jonathan, and made sure David was included in their warm welcome.

Two other guests were seated at the Hurvitzes long table in the community dining hall. One was a shy young man from Switzerland named Jan Hansen. The other, a man in his sixties, introduced himself as "Sam Finerman from Chicago." The eldest kibbutz member conducted the *seder* as the rest followed the service, drinking wine with matzoh, and eating bitter herbs and hard-boiled eggs in remembrance of their ancestors' struggle to reach the land of Israel. This was followed by a sweet concoction of finely diced apples, walnuts and dates, mixed with cinnamon and wine, called *haroset,* to commemorate the sweetness of their arrival.

Everyone in the kibbutz came over to greet them during the meal. It was obvious Gideon, being an Air Force pilot, was their pride and joy. Two kibbutzniks with guitars began to play music celebrating the Passover. People sang and danced in the aisles. Nilli and Ronit pulled the men up from the table, insisting they join in the dancing.

After they cleaned off their dishes and put them on a trolley which traveled back to the kitchen, the visitors gathered for coffee at the Hurvitzes. Although it was spring, the Galilee was damp and still cold at night. Gideon and Jonathan built a fire in the stone hearth while Ronit and Nilli helped Mrs. Hurvitz serve coffee. A platter of macaroons, fruit and nuts was placed on a small table that everyone huddled around while listening to Sam. He had lost many family members in the Holocaust and described himself as a staunch Zionist. He deplored those who were against Israel and the Jews. "Israel is the homeland for the Jews and we should never forget that."

Sam spoke of the rising anti-Semitism in America and asked Jan how things were for the Jews in Switzerland. Like David, Jan had never given much thought to how Jews were treated in his country. As far as he knew, they were treated like everyone else. His mother was a French Jew, his father a Lebanese Christian. They were both college professors who, as devout atheists, believed religion was for the poor and feeble-minded. Jan's curiosity about his parents' heritage had brought him to the Middle East to explore Lebanon and Israel.

Gideon and Sam moved on to American politics. Gideon asked him what he thought about President Johnson. Sam believed him to be an honorable man, but "he's no Truman," and questioned his policy toward Israel. "We'll just have to wait and see."

Sam then went on to speak of Roosevelt, how every American thought of him as a great president. But Sam despised him, calling him one of the worst anti-Semites in American history. Roosevelt had refused to grant visas to Jews during World War II, knowing full well what the Nazis were doing to them. Roosevelt, he said, had even turned away a refugee ship approaching the shores of America, allowing the Germans to bomb it, killing everyone on board.

He then told the story of a man he had befriended, named Harry Bingham. He had been in the diplomatic service in France before the United States entered the war, serving as the United States Consul in Marseilles. When Roosevelt ordered that Jews were not to be given visas, despite all the evidence about their persecution by the Nazis, Bingham decided the policy was immoral and, risking his career, did everything in his power to undermine it. He granted over twenty-five hundred United States visas to Jews and other refugees, including artists Marc Chagall, Max Ernst and the family of writer Thomas Mann. Bingham sheltered Jews in his home and obtained forged identity papers to help them in their dangerous journeys across Europe. He worked with the French underground to smuggle Jews out of France into Spain or across the Mediterranean, and contributed to their expenses out of his own pocket. In 1941, Washington sent Bingham to Argentina, where, after the war, he continued to annoy his superiors by reporting on the movements of Nazi war criminals. Harry Bingham was eventually forced out of the United States diplomatic service. Sam was in Israel to make certain Israel honored Bingham's heroism by formally recognizing him as a "righteous gentile." The conversation lasted past midnight, when they left for their guest rooms.

David lay awake in a room which had just enough space for a single bed and a standing lamp. His thoughts went back to

Safed, which he wanted to explore on his own as it had lit in him an unexpected curiosity about the mystical aspects of Judaism. He was also excited by the prospect of returning in June with Gideon for a hike down the Amud Valley. But Sam's Zionism left him unmoved. He listened to the clamor of crickets blaring against the silent backdrop of the countryside, before closing his eyes, imagining his next encounter with Tamar.

The *seder* ended late in the night, with Reb Eli placing his hands over his grandchildren's heads, and blessing each one as they came and stood before him. Grateful for his family, he sat back and listened as Sarah led everyone in singing the joyous songs of *Pesach.*

He heard a change in Sarah's voice. There were colors in it that he hadn't heard before. Although he could still hear her pain, she seemed to have come to a deeper maturity. The rebbe welcomed the transformation. Still, he could not stop wondering why his daughter avoided looking at him whenever she spoke. Something was amiss. Difficult as it was for him to accept, he knew there was nothing he could do but let God reveal Sarah's destiny in His own time.

Sarah called Madame Aziza telling her she could no longer be with the Englishman. Madame Aziza was taken by surprise, asking what was wrong and what she could do to resolve any difficulties. Sarah was not prepared to confess she was in love with the Englishman and was unable to bear that he thought of her as nothing more than a prostitute. She knew Madame Aziza was, above all else, a businesswoman.

Madame Aziza was persistent. If she would tell her what was bothering her, she promised to take care of it. When Sarah hesitated, she begged her not to renege on her commitment. She, after all, had invested so much in her, agreeing to her request that the Englishman be her only client, and not be told about it. What Madame Aziza said was true. How could she be upset that David thought her a prostitute when that was exactly what she wanted him to think. Realizing the absurdity of her position and longing to be with David, Sarah agreed to be at Madame Aziza's that Sunday night.

David was still asleep when Jonathan knocked on his door to ask if he would join him for breakfast in the dining hall.

The communal shower was occupied. He waited a few minutes before an attractive young woman wrapped in a white towel stepped out. In a matter-of-fact manner she said, "*boker tov,*" a greeting in Hebrew meaning "good morning," without taking much notice of him. He envied her nonchalance.

He showered, dressed and went to join Jonathan and Jan. Most of the kibbutzniks were already at their jobs. There were a few people cleaning up, as they sipped their coffee and talked about their restful night and how wonderfully simple kibbutz living was. Their reverie ended abruptly when a siren blared, warning of an imminent attack.

People came running from the kitchen yelling, "Run, run to the shelter!" As they ran from the dining hall, a blast hit it. Time and sound evaporated into surreal, slow motion as the building crumbled with particles scattering everywhere. The room was filled with smoke and white dust. Everything became blurred and strangely quiet. Tamar's face flashed before him, when a sudden cry brought him back. Jan had been struck in the thigh by a piece of shrapnel. He fell to the ground shrieking in pain. Jonathan and David lifted him and carried him to the shelter. Outside the dining hall, parents ran to gather their children in the nursery and school; others ran towards the shelters, screaming. Within seconds, the entire kibbutz had become a war zone.

They took shelter in a damp underground bunker, along with Sam, the Hurvitzes and some elderly people who were huddled together. The shelling seemed endless. Sam muttered, "This is the story of the Jews."

The infirmary had been shelled and it was impossible to get to the medical supplies. The shrapnel was deeply embedded and Jan was in terrible pain. The nearest hospital was twenty kilometers away.

David's immediate shock at the attack had worn off. Now, he felt helpless and claustrophobic, hiding in the shelter, not knowing when the shelling was going to stop. The smoke and dust were burning his eyes and throat. The sound of shells falling drowned out Jan's moans. David felt awful. There was nothing they could do for him. David didn't have much tolerance for pain and thought what if it were he who had been hit. When the shelling seemed to have ended, Nilli asked her father if all the kibbutz vehicles still had their keys left in them for emergencies. He said, "Yes, of course. The attacks keep coming."

David decided to run for the nearest car so he could take Jan to the hospital. Before anyone could stop him, he was out and running. A few hundred feet from the shelter, he heard the roar of an incoming shell, then the explosion. He stood frozen, not knowing what to do, when he saw Gideon rushing toward him in his Volkswagen, shouting, "Get in!" Gideon took charge, driving up close to the shelter. Running into it, he lifted Jan over his shoulder and carried him to the back seat, accompanied by David, Jonathan and Nilli.

He handed Nilli a bottle of Passover wine. "Have him drink this to dull the pain." He handed his keys to David. "Can you drive fast?"

"Yes, as fast as this car can go."

"Good. Nilli will direct you to the hospital. I need to stay here."

"Has anyone else been hurt?" David asked.

"By some miracle, no."

David had never felt such relief and gratitude. He sped down the mountain as Jonathan and Nilli comforted Jan in the back seat. They reached the hospital in less than half an hour, in time to save Jan's swollen leg.

Two hundred shells had fallen on the kibbutz. Most of the structures, including the Hurvitzes home, were damaged. The chicken sheds were destroyed and all the chickens killed, but, thanks to the early warning of the siren, there had been no human casualties. Neighboring Kibbutzim were also hit and their livestock killed. And many shells had fallen into Lake Kinneret, killing large numbers of fish.

After all-day artillery duels and the downing of six Mig-21s by the Israeli Air Force, the Syrians called it a day at five o'clock. By nightfall hundreds of volunteers arrived from neighboring villages and kibbutzim, bringing food and supplies and standing ready to help repair the damage.

The Hurvitzes refused to leave. They had been attacked many times before, especially in the last two years. This had become normal for them. The kibbutz was their home and nothing would make them leave it. Gideon and Ronit decided to stay with them until they were settled. Sam, too, insisted on staying to help. David knew staying and helping out in the kibbutz was the right thing for him to do as well. Jonathan and Nilli apologized for being obliged to return to Jerusalem. Nilli had to be on duty at the hospital and Jonathan needed to return to his studies. Gideon assured Nilli and Jonathan not to worry, there was enough help coming into the kibbutz, and insisted David return with them as well.

"There's so much damage, surely you could use another hand," David offered.

"Thank you, but we're fine. We're used to picking up the rubble and rebuilding our houses. We just make them that much stronger after every attack," Gideon said.

David nodded. As he said, "I'll see you back in Jerusalem," he was ashamed for feeling so relieved to be leaving.

Sarah's menstruation came early. In accordance with the religious laws of *needa,* she needed to be clean for seven days before she could be with a man. She would have to tell Madame Aziza to postpone her rendezvous with David. Not even her passion for him would make her forsake the laws of *needa.*

There was no law forbidding an unmarried woman from being with an unmarried man, but she was troubled by her pretense to be a prostitute, even though it was not causing harm to another and she had made certain no one would ever find out about it. Wasn't it still trickery? After all, David was paying Madame Aziza to be with her. And just because she did not accept money or intend harm to anyone did not mean she hadn't broken a law. She feared if, by omitting the truth about who she really was, she had forsaken a teaching of the Torah. She certainly could not inquire about such a case from her father. Her charade began to disturb her. She knew how ridiculous it was to be heartbroken that her pretense had worked. Nonetheless, it pained her that David did not love her as she loved him. She became swept away by her fears, guilt and regret. She was certain to be held liable for her transgression. She prayed, in the sacred time of *Pesach,* that God would know, in her heart, she meant no harm to anyone, and promised to stop if God would be merciful in his judgment.

David's phone rang late in the morning. It was Madame Aziza apologizing that Tamar was not feeling well and would not be available that evening and would he mind terribly if they made the same arrangement for the following week?

David, still in a somber mood from the attack on the kibbutz, politely agreed, but after he hung up he felt humiliated and angry. Did Madame Aziza and Tamar take him for a fool? Didn't they realize he could figure out Tamar had received a better offer for the night? How dare they think he was so naïve and stupid? This, he told himself, is the kind of insult you receive when you allow yourself to get involved with a prostitute. He wanted to call back and tell Madame Aziza he would let her know if and when it next suited him to see Tamar. Instead he called the rebbe, asking if he could see him later in the afternoon.

Sarah was in good spirits preparing the afternoon tea. She arranged the tray carefully, just the way her father liked it, with a piping hot teapot in a caddy, a small jug of milk beside it, and English tea biscuits. She was about to enter her father's study when she heard David's voice inside. Panic-stricken and trembling, she dropped the tray. The teapot, cup and saucer crashed to the floor, splattering tea, milk and biscuits everywhere. She ran back into the kitchen where Miriam and Esther were preparing dinner. Looking pale and ill, she told her sisters she was struck with severe cramps and had to lie down. She apologized for the mess she had made and asked if they would mind cleaning up. Esther became worried that Sarah should be taken to the hospital. Sarah, shaking, assured her she just needed to go and lie down with a hot water bottle.

Miriam didn't quite believe Sarah, who was fine just a minute ago. There was something suspicious about how nervous she was. Ignoring Sarah's sense of urgency, when she asked her to "please bring father his tea," Miriam responded with annoyance, "After I clean up, I'll bring him his tea."

Shortly after hearing a crash outside his study, there was a knock on the door. Miriam brought in the tray and placed it on the table before the rebbe. He rarely had visitors during his afternoon tea. He usually spent the time alone, reading or visiting with Sarah, who always brought it to him.

He looked at Miriam, concerned. "Is everything all right?" he asked in Hebrew, to keep the matter private.

"Everything is fine. Sarah is not feeling well, she has cramps," she said, somewhat annoyed. The rebbe asked her to please bring in another cup for his guest.

Miriam, who was a married woman, made certain to be physically unobtrusive before a man. She placed the cup on the tray and quickly left for the kitchen, where she asked Esther why the Englishman was visiting during the rebbe's afternoon tea. Esther was as surprised as Miriam and decided, "it must be an urgent matter."

The rebbe listened carefully as David relayed the story of the attack on the kibbutz and the guilt and shame he felt for not insisting on staying, confessing it was because of his desire to be with Tamar. How disappointed and angry he was to have returned to be with her, only to be given some questionable excuse by Madame Aziza for having to postpone his appointment.

Reb Eli had a growing concern that he had made a mistake arranging for David to go to the House. He had hoped if he got help with his problem it would free him of his inhibitions with women; never had he imagined David would become so enamored with one of Madame Aziza's girls.

The rebbe remembered his own youth, how aroused he had become when, at fifteen, living in England, he first saw the bare ankle of a young woman as she walked down the street; how enticed he had become by the slender shape of her ankle. His mind had become filled with thoughts he felt ashamed to admit, even to himself. Those raw sensuous feelings were now a thing of the past for him. Having watched the agonizing death of his wife, his sexual appetite had changed into a hunger for the wisdom of Torah and the Kabbalah. Intimacy and personal love were reserved for his children and grandchildren and his close community. This, he discovered, was a sound foundation for relationships, these feelings were sustainable and nourished people; carnality was short lived, unless it translated into a deeper, meaningful connection, one that included love and awe for the divine.

Reb Eli cautioned David about visiting the House any further. It would be best for him not to dwell on his thoughts about Tamar. He must choose wisely before allowing emotions to overtake him as it was not prudent to submit to such a hopeless situation. The rebbe assured David he would find a woman who would be flattered to be given so much attention. His desires, the rebbe said, were a sign he was ready to meet his *beshert.* He suggested that perhaps returning home would bring a broader perspective to his feelings. Afterwards, when this infatuation subsided, he could return to Jerusalem.

FIVE

Sarah climbed the steps to see Madame Aziza. Tonight, she decided, would be the last time she would be with David. She would thank Madame Aziza for all she had taught her and say good-bye.

Madame Aziza was delighted to see her. She had interesting news to share. The Englishman had called to announce he was returning home and didn't know when or if he would be returning. He had a special request: Would she consider paying him a final visit at his flat in Abu Tor?

Hearing of David's leaving, Sarah felt as though her stomach had been turned inside out. The news took her by surprise and she said, simply, "I'm sorry, that's not possible."

"He's already paid handsomely and provided for a taxi to pick you up here and return you as well."

"It's best I don't see the Englishman anymore."

Madame Aziza, with a motherly manner, inquired what was troubling her.

"I've come to realize, I'm unable to do this," she confessed.

"Tamar, have I not treated you well and respected your privacy?"

"You have been very kind and generous with me, as I have been with you," Sarah said, straightforwardly.

"I am asking you to please respect our agreement as a final gesture of trust and goodwill and go to him this last time."

When Sarah did not answer, Madame Aziza stated, in a whisper of quiet menace, "You have my word I will keep secret all that has been between us."

The weather had turned warm and the smell of honeysuckle permeated the night air. Outside on the rooftop, David could smell its sweetness. He looked out over the city with its sparse, flickering lights.

Earlier in the afternoon, he had gone to the *macholet* to buy wine and Shabbat candles, as they were the only ones available for his evening rendezvous with Tamar. He lit the candles throughout the flat and out on the roof. The transformation delighted him. He knew that having Tamar come to his place would give him an opportunity to experience her on his turf without the frills of Madame Aziza's. He was confident her appeal would be less enticing without the House's alluring ambience. Thinking perhaps the candles would obscure his purpose in having Tamar come to his flat, he extinguished them. Ten minutes later, he decided to light them again.

As the time grew closer to her arrival, he poured himself a glass of wine. Tonight, he told himself, was the last time he would indulge in a fantasy. He had learned a lot in Jerusalem. Now it was time to move on.

When he opened the door and saw Tamar standing before him in her green dress, carrying a small black purse, he was glad he had decided to re-light the candles. Once again, his desire to hold her and smell her essence was interrupted with a polite greeting.

Sarah tried to squelch the pain in the pit of her stomach. She wished she had been stronger in her refusal to come and not been so intimidated by Madame Aziza. Seeing David, and knowing this was her last time to be with him, made her heartsick.

Outside on the roof, the candles flickered in the gentle breeze. She looked out at the shimmering lights of the city. In the distance, the King David Hotel stood perched high on the hill. Her mind traveled back to when, as a little girl of four, she had accompanied her father there at night to visit a friend of his from England. The man was immaculately dressed in a dark pinstripe suit. He was kindly and had brought her a huge box of Swiss chocolates that he presented out on the hotel's terrace, which was lit up by the stars and moon. Sarah had imagined she, too, was a bright star hovering high above, one that could travel to faraway places. How enthralled she had been by that visit. What she did not know or remember was that her father's friend had been Phillip Bennett.

Tonight, standing on the rooftop with David, the city appeared even more beautiful. She was awestruck by the way the moon shone over the ancient monuments, making them appear mysterious and magical. She felt ancestral souls suspended in the ethereal realm, and wondered what secrets they held.

Sipping wine from the glass David held to her lips, she saw him look at her with an intensity she had not seen before. There was something in his eyes that was more than just desire, a yearning, a beckoning.

He stood behind her, nuzzling her hair and neck. "Enchanting, isn't it?"

"Yes. In your travels, were there any cities as beautiful as this?"

"Not in the same way." Overwhelmed by desire, he turned

her toward him. Her eyes glistened brightly, as intoxicating and mysterious as the city behind them.

"Why did you ask for me to come here?" she asked.

"So I could see if you are as beautiful as I imagine."

David kissed her, then disrobed her until she stood naked before him.

His words had both ignited Sarah's heart and made it ache with sorrow, for this would be the last time she would see him, the last time she would know what passion lay in her body and heart. When this night was over, she would return to the solemn rituals of her life, keeping her love a secret to be treasured forever. For a moment in time, her heart had danced with liberating joy. Her gift from God was short, but sublime. Sarah knew she would no longer leave this earth with an empty hand.

Like two dancers in tune to each other's rhythm and touch, Sarah and David surrendered to their passion, not knowing how their destiny would unfold.

It was long before sunrise when the taxi returned Sarah to Madame Aziza's house. Hurrying toward the bus station, the deserted Machane Yehuda souk felt eerie. She could think only of David, her entire being exalted with a poignant love she could barely contain.

Changing quickly in the lavatory, she discovered the thousand-pound bonus David had neatly placed in her black purse. The money ripped through her heart. The love she felt from him was an illusion. She knew now he simply thought her nothing more than a whore who satisfied his needs. She wept until she could weep no more.

The sudden change in Sarah bewildered Reb Eli. Just when he thought she had overcome her grief, she had once again become sullen. She spoke little and, on Shabbat, when she sang, her voice was tired and empty. The rest of the family felt her despair had returned, and became concerned. The rebbe tried to comfort them, as well as himself, explaining Sarah must have had a relapse, and they should trust that, in time, all would be well again.

The next evening, Sarah had not come down to join her family for dinner. The family listened eagerly, as it was a rarity that the rebbe spoke of anyone, nameless or otherwise, unless it was to reveal the mystery of *Hashem*. Reb Eli told of a young woman who, two weeks previously, had come to him in deep anguish. After three years of marriage, she had been unable to conceive, and her husband had insisted on a divorce. She loved her husband and was inconsolable. The woman told the rebbe of a fertility doctor in Paris who had helped many women to conceive. She begged the rebbe to help her see this doctor. Mindful of his own daughter's dilemma with being barren, which he did not mention, the rebbe felt compelled to do all he could to raise the money. He asked from all those he knew to give generously so a *mitzvah* could be performed, but the rising tension with Egypt had captured everyone's attention. They were focused on their own insecurity, so they gave very little. The rebbe confided how he had become despondent over his inability to do more for her.

Yesterday, just before Shabbat, when he went to check the *seducah* box, a little more than fifty pounds was in it. This evening, he had an inclination to once again check the *seducah* box. There, as never before, was a one-thousand-pound note! "A miracle, *mertz Hashem.*"

From the moment David arrived in England, he knew going home was a mistake. His longing for Tamar was now deeper, with an intensity that made his emptiness ache without mercy. All he could think about was Tamar, his beautiful, wondrous, sensual whore. Clinging to the memory of her face, her smell, her touch, his body mourned for her. He regretted his promise to Reb Eli and Jonathan that he would return to England and free himself from her. He tried to shield his anguish by hiding behind his mannered veneer, presenting himself as a well-bred Englishman, devoid of emotion.

Nothing much had changed in the Bennett household. Dinner was served promptly at eight o'clock to polite conversation. Tonight, in honor of his return, Victoria Bennett had invited several family members and their friends for a celebration. Two more staff were added to serve drinks, while a harpist played Baroque music. Phillip Bennett behaved like a proud father welcoming his heroic son back from a third world adventure. He was witty and affable as he chatted with his guests. David's alienation from this pantomime of "gracious living," as his mother liked to call it, was now more apparent than ever.

David's Aunt Eleanor noticed how distracted he was throughout the evening. She knew him well and could tell something was wrong. Brandy was served after dinner. David, who had had more than his share of wine and port, was drinking the brandy hoping it would relieve his despondency, when

Eleanor joined him on the settee. He always enjoyed the company of his Aunt Eleanor. For as long as he could remember, they had shared a tender intimacy. Eleanor and Jonathan were his closest family members. They accepted his oddities and were always available for him. There were many times when David had wondered what he would have done without them.

"How are you?"

David smiled as best he could.

Eleanor repeated her inquiry, "Honestly now, how are you?"

"Not very well, I'm afraid."

"Did you not enjoy your visit to Israel?"

"It's a bit complicated," David confessed.

"I would imagine that suited you well."

"On the contrary, I'm quite baffled about it, not sure I understand it at all."

"It's good to have you home. I've missed you terribly. It was difficult enough having Jonathan gone."

Eleanor's words embraced him like a warm, cozy blanket in a winter storm. At that moment, it was what he desperately needed. He leaned over and kissed her tenderly on the cheek.

"If it's any consolation, Jonathan is quite happy and doing well. Nilli is lovely."

"So I've heard," Eleanor said, happily.

She remained quiet. Her eyes searched David's, waiting for him to find the right moment to tell her what was troubling him. She had a way of making him feel that anything he shared with her would attract no judgment and be kept in confidence.

David tried to divert his aunt's attention from himself and spoke of Reb Eli.

"The rebbe is a wonderful man, quite an inspiration."

"Apparently you and he hit it off quite well. Why did you come home?"

"I had to," David admitted.

"Let's enjoy our brandy in the conservatory," she suggested.

Alone in the conservatory, Eleanor listened carefully to David's dilemma about Tamar. He did not mention how or why he had gone to a bordello.

"I don't mean to sound like a lovesick school boy, but being with her, her sensitivity, the way she seemed to know everything I wanted or felt, without ever an exchange of words, everything about her is beyond any words I can possibly describe."

Eleanor remained reflective for some time, searching for the words that would give him strength and guidance.

"Strange how, when we least expect it and, at times, in the most peculiar way, our hearts are opened. Perhaps this young woman was a blessing, something to remember and cherish ... until you find that passion again."

"I don't think I ever will," David replied.

Although Eleanor didn't believe it, she said, "Of course, you will."

"Have you?" he asked, wondering why she hadn't remarried after Jonathan's father died years ago.

She could not find it within herself to confess who had been her first and lasting love. She needed to give David hope. "It's not easy as you grow older, but you're young. All of life is before you. The difficulty is in the waiting. Be patient," she said, comfortingly, wishing she could believe it to be true.

During May, the first song birds had arrived, announcing the warmer weather. Sweet scents of spring permeated the Bennett's estate. The gardens were alive with blossoms, and yellow buttercups dotted the hills.

On an afternoon when the morning drizzle had given way to a glorious sunny day, and the smell of the first fresh-cut grass filled the air, David lay on the bank of the river, soaking up the sun. His mind drifted back to when he and Jonathan would ride their bicycles along the path, sheltering under the willow trees from rain showers that came and went all summer long. The music of the river, as it flowed around rocks in its stream, lulled him into a deep sleep.

He woke with a sense of foreboding. He brushed the dust from his clothes, as though that would lighten his mood, but he could not shake off the dread he was feeling, and headed home.

Tea was being served in the parlor as Phillip read aloud from *The Times*. David and his mother listened quietly.

> *Nasser has ordered the UN Emergency Force, which has been stationed in the Sinai since 1956, to withdraw, without bringing the matter to the attention of the General Assembly, as his predecessor had promised. Secretary-General U Thant has complied with the demand. This morning, Egypt moved troops into the Sinai, massing on the Israeli border. Syrian troops have assembled along the Golan Heights, prepared for war.*

Phillip put down the paper. He stood staring at it. "They're planning to destroy Israel."

Trying to remain calm, Victoria said, "That would be madness. Surely the world won't sit back and allow that to happen."

"I wouldn't be so sure," Phillip said worriedly.

Tension ran high at the Israeli Embassy in London. Staff nervously bustled about trying to answer the flood of incoming calls. David had met the Ambassador before, at a fund-raising dinner his father had presided over. He had found him to be a poised, cordial man. Today, he could hear anxiety in his voice. He looked harrowed as he spoke to his father. "The Egyptians have closed the Straits of Tiran, blockading all shipping bound for Eilat."

"Why?"

"To cripple our route to Iran so that our main supply of oil is cut off."

"What does Nasser want?" Phillip asked, trying to grasp all that was happening.

"His exact words were 'The extermination of Zionist existence.' Assad has jumped in as well. He's promising to 'explode the Zionist presence in the Arab homeland,' and that his Syrian army is 'ready to enter into a battle of annihilation.' We're doing our best through diplomatic channels. Abba Ebban is meeting with the Prime Minister as we speak."

The Ambassador, too weary for pretense, looked at Phillip. "Frankly, I don't have much hope with Wilson, nor with the Americans either, not with that *momzer* Rusk advising Johnson."

Phillip shook his head, "This doesn't make sense... Britain guaranteed Israel's freedom of navigation."

"So did France. They've reneged on their commitments, Phillip. It's the same old story. When all is said and done, nobody gives a damn about the Jews."

"I'll do all I can to raise what's needed." Phillip promised.

"I know you will." The ambassador nodded his head in gratitude. "Thank you."

Heavy rain was falling outside their house on Chesham Place in Belgravia as David watched his father drink his second scotch and water while they followed the television news reporting on the buildup against Israel.

David had heard his father say many times that Jews should never forget the Holocaust or the indifference of the world in the face of it. "Israel is the Jews' only guaranteed refuge." He relied on it as his safety net.

As soon as they arrived home, Phillip had turned on the television. They watched the news anchor describe the crisis in the Middle East, warning that "the tension continues to escalate. Israeli forces have been on alert for weeks, as the armies of Egypt, Syria and Jordan mobilize for war."

Phillip picked up the phone to call Jonathan. Israel was only an hour ahead. He heard the weariness in Jonathan's voice as he answered. He urged him to come home until things settled down. Jonathan tried to calm his uncle by telling him he was in good hands and knew what precautions to take in the event of war. But Philip could hear the apprehension in his voice, even as he asked him to assure his mother he would be fine. He was still hoping and praying for a peaceful outcome.

Jonathan's father had been on a business trip in Paris when a drunk driver killed him instantly. Jonathan had been twelve years old. His father's death had broken his heart and he had been inconsolable. Phillip had taken it upon himself to become his nephew's surrogate father. He had made certain his sister and nephew were always well looked after. Jonathan remaining in Israel at a time like this made him terribly anxious and he was unable to sleep. Although Jonathan was now a man of twenty-eight, he felt the same responsibility for his well-being as for his own son. Too tired to think, he told himself he would deal with this first thing in the morning.

At seven in the morning, he awoke to a note on his night table.

Dad, Returned to Israel. Will be in touch. No need to worry—I'm not the heroic type.

David

SIX

Kupat Holim's medical center was always crowded. This morning, it was packed beyond capacity. The threat of war weighed heavily on everyone, causing their symptoms, including those only imagined, to intensify.

Sarah had arrived before the doors opened at seven o'clock, hoping she would not have to wait long to see the doctor, as she needed to be back in time to teach her class. She was certain her heartbreak over David and the weeks of stress caused by the talk of war were the cause of her maladies, but memories of her mother's illness and Yossi's initial symptoms made her want to see Dr. Cooper just in case and to dispel her fears.

Dr. Shoshana Cooper was the established "woman's doctor" to many of the Hasidic women. Now in her sixties, she was old enough to be looked upon as a mother figure by the younger generation. The older women, including Sarah's deceased mother, had always regarded her as a confidante. Sarah had been under her care during her three years of marriage when she had been unable to conceive. Dr. Cooper could not find a cause for her infertility and assigned it to the unknown. The doctor was a quiet woman who spoke only when necessary. Her warm, gentle manner invited trust, and her patients felt free to share their deepest thoughts and feelings with her.

A week prior to this morning's visit, Sarah had been to see Dr. Cooper, whose mere touch of hands helped soothe her anxiety. After examining Sarah, she ordered urine and blood samples to be sent to the laboratory. She had suggested Sarah return in a week's time so they could go over the results together.

Sarah sat in stunned silence. The cheerful, assured manner with which Dr. Cooper had delivered her diagnosis made her feel she was living in a surreal world. It was only when she repeated her diagnosis that she was able to take it in.

"Sarah, the tests confirm my examination. You're pregnant."

From the moment David's feet touched the ground at Lod Airport, he could smell and feel Tamar. The country was facing a devastating war and he could think only of her. His thoughts shamefully aroused him.

"I'm here to help in any way I can," David replied, after Jonathan had asked why he had come back. "David, this isn't a time to be frivolous. There is too much at stake," Jonathan warned.

"Don't you think I realize that?"

"I certainly hope so."

"Any word if the U.S. negotiations are working?" David asked, hoping to ease their tension.

"I wouldn't count on that. Nasser has created a frenzy that's out of control. He couldn't stop it even if he wanted to."

Driving silently back to Jerusalem, Jonathan was more anxious than David had ever seen him. Embedded along the road on the outskirts of the city were the remains of rusted army vehicles, memorials to those who had died fighting in the War of Independence. David felt queasy thinking of how many would die if war broke out.

To block out any light that might be spotted by enemy planes, and to keep the glass windows and doors from splattering,

David and Jonathan carefully finished taping David's flat with dark blue tape, a task performed across the entire country, in preparation for war. Nilli, Jonathan told him, was on twenty-four-hour call at Hadassah Hospital. Other than the gravely ill, the hospital had been evacuated to make room for wounded soldiers. Anat's unit had been deployed to the Golan, where there was a large mobilization of Arab forces.

After weeks of duty, the Air Force had given Gideon an eight-hour pass. He and Ronit were on their way back from seeing his parents at the kibbutz. Tonight, at Jonathan's request, Gideon had arranged for David and him to work as volunteer drivers so that soldiers could be relieved to prepare for the anticipated ground battle in Jerusalem.

At dusk, Gideon drove them to a makeshift warehouse on a hilltop on the outskirts of the city. Gideon's friend, a young lieutenant called Yair Peretz, welcomed them. Yair offered them coffee before giving them instructions on emergency maneuvers. While they gulped down the muddy Turkish coffee, Gideon spoke rapidly with Yair in Hebrew. He patted Jonathan on the arm. "See you soon, take care."

"I'll look after Nilli," Jonathan said, reassuringly.

"I know." He looked at David, "It's good to have you with us."

David choked back his emotions. "Thank you."

When he and Jonathan walked Gideon out to his car, all David could say was, "take care."

Jonathan tried hard to hold back his fear. His mouth quivered when he hugged Gideon good-bye.

"Don't worry. Whatever happens, know we Jews are the

resurrection." Gideon then sped off in his old Volkswagen, leaving behind a trail of smoke and dust.

After their briefing, they were sent to Hadassah Hospital's emergency ward. All the staff were glued to the non-stop news on television. King Hussein of Jordan was speaking stridently in Arabic, as Hebrew and English subtitles interpreted.

> *The armies of Egypt, Jordan, Syria and Lebanon are poised on the borders of Israel ... to face the challenge. Standing behind us are the armies of Iraq, Algeria, Kuwait, Sudan and the whole Arab nation. This military action will astound the world. Today, they will know the Arabs are ready for battle; the critical hour has arrived. We have gone past the time of declarations to the stage of action." Then President Abdur Rahman Aref of Iraq appeared, joining in the war talk: "The existence of Israel is an error which must be rectified. This is our opportunity to wipe out the ignominy which has been with us since 1948. Our goal is clear—to wipe Israel off the map.*

Seconds later, America's President Lyndon B. Johnson appeared, declaring, "Israel will not be alone unless it decides to go alone."

No one in the emergency room spoke or looked at one another. The air was too filled with tension. David hated feeling like a sitting duck, waiting for the slaughter.

Jonathan put his arm around Nilli, "You know how they like to whip up this rubbish."

"Yes, and how many of our boys will fall because of it."

Sitting around, waiting for war, day after day, became more and more harrowing. David, like all the hospital staff and volunteers, drank coffee endlessly and watched the television news obsessively.

To fill in the details, he read the *Jerusalem Post*.

The weather turned hot. Though it was barely a week since he had returned to Israel, it already felt like he had been there for an eternity. As a volunteer, he was free to come and go as he pleased, but he felt compelled to spend as much time as he could at the hospital. He constantly yearned for relief from the threat of war.

Sullen from listening to the continuous news reports on the radio, Madame Aziza sipped her honey and orange-water tea, "If you warm your insides, the heat won't affect you as much," she remembered her mother saying during the oppressive summers in Egypt.

She wished she knew how to stop the fire in her blood from raging. Once again, she had to endure Nasser's threats to rid himself of the Jews. This time would be different. This time she was on her own land and neither Nasser nor the entire Arab world would force her from her country. If need be, she would fight to the death.

She closed her eyes, resting her head against the soft velvet chair, listening to Umm Kulthum's songs of love and life which, since her youth, had soothed and embraced her whenever she felt any ache in her heart. When the doorbell rang, it jolted her out of her respite.

No clients had been by for two weeks. Most of the young

men had been called to duty, and the Hasidim chose to spend this time of dread in prayer. The doorbell continued to ring. She got up to answer it, thinking whoever was at the door must have very strong urges that even an impending war could not deter.

"May I please come in?" David asked, apologetically.

"You have returned. It's good to see you."

Given the state everyone in the country was in, Madame Aziza seemed happy to see him. He was surprised by her warm welcome.

David confessed his feelings about Tamar, telling her he could no longer ignore them. He asked if it was possible to see her. She told him that, due to the crisis, her house was closed for business.

"Do you have any idea where I can find her?" David asked, trying not to sound desperate.

"I have no information where she lives or even a telephone number where she can be reached," she said, truthfully.

David asked cautiously if perhaps one of her clients or the other ladies would be privy to that information.

"I doubt it."

"Are you certain?"

At that moment, she wanted to tell David the truth about his being Tamar's only client, that Tamar had specifically asked for him and had never accepted any of his money. Life, after all, was fragile and no one knew what tomorrow would bring. Why not give this young man who had fallen in love the truth? But she knew the promise she had made to Tamar and intended to keep it. It was, after all, not her job to be a matchmaker.

"In the event I hear from her, I will call you. Other than that, I have no way of contacting her."

Sarah chewed the salted cracker, hoping it would relieve her nausea. She prayed for strength to overcome it so she could teach her class without bringing attention to herself. She prayed the American negotiations with the Arabs would work. War was now an unbearable thought. Since discovering her pregnancy, she had been unable to sleep. She lay awake night after night, mulling over what to do. She knew she would have to leave Mea Shearim to find a place where she could make a new life for herself and her child. She also knew the shame and pain this would cause her father and family. But right now, all she could think about was the gripping nausea. She took another bite of the salted cracker, smiled at all the young adoring girls in her class, and continued with the day's lesson.

Each morning, Reb Eli led the men in prayer, praying for peace in Israel and the entire world. The rebbe prayed with all his heart that war should not come. He, like so many others, had witnessed enough wars. *Why, Eloheim, do so many feel threatened by our existence?* he heard his heart cry out. *Sh'ma Yisrael, Adonai elohenu, Adonai ehad.*

In the quiet of his study, he sought to understand the Arabs' barrage of hatred. Surely the Jews could not pose such a threat to them? Perhaps the truth lay in a deeper cause. He imagined how it would have been in biblical times if Abraham had not obeyed Sarah's demand to send away Hagar and Hagar's son, Ishmael. Could there have been one nation, with no need to fight over which of the women's sons was the favorite of their father? Had this ancestral rejection become so deeply ingrained in the Arabs' fabric that they needed to prove themselves worthy by killing their half-brothers? *God of Abraham, how can we reach out for peace so we can heal their pain?* he silently asked.

The rebbe struggled to understand why there was so much hatred of the Jews. Did the Christians oppress them because their faith in Jesus was so fragile? Did the gentiles not know Jesus was a Jew, like all those they murdered?

The sound of sirens startled David out of his sleep. They continued to wail loudly. He reached for the light switch to see what time it was and discovered there was no electricity. He ran out to the roof.

The early heat of the day could already be felt on the rooftop. The morning sky was a sparkling clear blue, with soft white clouds floating peacefully across the sun. A thunderous roar came from the Jordanian side of Jerusalem's hills as an artillery shell hit the house across the road. The blue taped windows shattered, and fragments of stones began to crumble as more of the same sound boomed over the city. David stood frozen with disbelief. Below, a woman with her children still dressed in their night clothes came running out into the street. The woman looked up and cried out, "War! War!" Within seconds, the street was filled with women, children and the elderly running toward the shelter at the end of the road.

The smell of sweat and dampness aggravated Sarah's nausea. The over-crowded, windowless shelter was packed.

She sat with her sisters, sisters-in-law and their children. The night had brought no relief to the heat and mugginess. Running up and down the stairs all day in the continuous air-raid drills had left her weak and ill, but she dared not feel sorry for herself when so many young men were risking their lives fighting for their country. She feared how many had already been injured or killed and wondered how long this war would last. She dreaded what would happen if the Arabs won. It had been less than twenty-four hours since the war began and she was sick with fear. The shelling had continued day and night. In the shelter, a small radio brought the news.

Israel's national broadcaster gave little information, just codes directing soldiers to their posts. On the Egyptian station, an announcer described how Arab troops were advancing on Tel Aviv. President Nasser and King Hussein boasted, "Victory will soon be ours. Jerusalem will soon be unified under the Jordanian flag. The Jews will be keeping company with the fishes in the sea."

Sarah was unable to hear any more. Ignoring the scolding and warnings of her sisters, she left the shelter to return to her flat, desperate to find a moment of quiet and peace. Lying down on her bed, she pulled the sheet over her head and prayed for the war to end.

The jeep was splattered with blood. As a makeshift ambulance, there was no time to clean it up. Every hour, more wounded soldiers were being carried in from the battlefield. David and Jonathan worked feverishly, driving between the hospital and the front lines. Medics administered emergency care long enough to get the soldiers transferred to Hadassah Hospital, where teams of doctors and nurses awaited the casualties. Helicopters flew continuously back and forth, picking up the most seriously hurt.

The hospital had been hit by Jordanian artillery and there was chaos as their jeep was replenished with medical supplies to transfer to the battlefield. Like everyone else, they drank black coffee and worked round the clock. The coffee kicked up their adrenalin to the point where they were unaware how numb and exhausted they had become. There was no time to think about how much longer it would go on. The hospital had no relief staff. Everyone had already been deployed.

The Knesset and university had also been hit, adding to the civilian casualties. At the emergency ward, Nilli worked as though every soldier's life depended solely on her. She avoided making eye contact with David or Jonathan.

The tourniquet tied just above the soldier's knee was soaked in blood. His leg had been blown off and he was in shock. David lay on a gurney ready to donate another pint of his O Negative blood. Since his blood type made him a universal donor, he was giving his second pint in two days. He closed his eyes, welcoming the relief of just lying there, when a sickening sensation hit him. He felt suddenly cowardly compared to the men fighting to save their country, losing arms, legs, eyes and their lives. How could he find respite in lying there, just giving blood? When juice was offered, he drank it quickly, insisting he was ready to return to his transport duty.

Outside, the cool night air eased his queasiness. Jonathan

noticed his face was ashen and asked him if he was okay.

"I'm fine. Let's go."

They jumped into the jeep, loaded with medical supplies and water, and headed down the hill back to the fighting.

Having returned to her sisters in the shelter, Sarah realized that she no longer belonged in their world, with its confined role for women. There could be no going back. Her thoughts were disrupted by a piercing roar, followed by an explosion. She instinctively ran into the street. As far as she could see, none of the houses were hit, but a plume of smoke was rising nearby. As sirens blared, she ran toward it, hugging the buildings for shelter. Reaching Rehov Straus, she saw a two story stone house in ruins. There was rubble everywhere. Those who had managed to escape were bloodied and dazed. Two older men desperately tried to dig through the wreckage. Sarah asked if there was anyone trapped inside.

"The Levis. The wife's disabled."

She joined the men in the rescue, until they were able to get to the doorway where a middle-aged man lay moaning, bleeding from a head wound. His wife was on the ground a few feet away, in shock. The two men lifted her out into the street. Not having anything available to stop the man's bleeding, Sarah pulled down her slip. On the back of her slip she saw stains of blood. Struck with panic, she took hold of herself, folded the slip and pressed it as hard as she could against the man's wound. Relieved to hear an ambulance approaching, she took his hand into hers and whispered the *Refuah Sh'lemah,* the prayer for health and healing, as much for him as for herself.

Lying in bed, Sarah raised her legs above her head, hoping to stop the bleeding. She prayed with all she possessed that she would not lose her baby. She cried out, begging for God's love and mercy. She committed herself before *Hashem* to do more *mitzvot* if He would hear and grant her prayer.

As her despair deepened, a light of hope appeared when she remembered her sister Esther had "spotted" with her last child. Dr. Cooper had ordered her to bed until it stopped. She promised herself that, no matter how many artillery shells fell on Jerusalem, she would not move until there was no more blood. The air raid siren sounded. She covered her ears.

Dvorah came running in from the shelter demanding to know why she was lying in bed. Sarah told her she was menstruating and not feeling well. She was too tired and ill to be running down to the shelter anymore. Dvorah insisted she return at once. "You'll get killed lying here! You have to come down."

"I can't." Then quickly, so her sister would cease arguing and leave, she stated firmly, "*Hashem* will protect me. Please let me rest here. As soon as I'm feeling better, I'll join you."

"I can't allow you to stay here," Dvorah said, in the same tone she had used since their mother died, whenever she felt the need to reprimand her.

"You can't force me to go down there."

"What if a shell hits the house?"

"I will die peacefully."

Dvorah reached into her pocket, pulled out a knife and handed it to her. "Take this in case it's true they're winning.

You know what they do to Jewish women."

Sarah was terrified by the thought. Knowing she would be unable to kill herself that way, she begged Dvorah to bring her some poison instead.

Throughout the shelling, Reb Eli continued to pray with the elders. The younger Hasidic men had decided to fight alongside the secular Jews. "What good is there in being alive if Israel should be defeated?" they argued.

Tonight, the rebbe felt like a five-thousand-year-old Jew. He argued with God, *"How many times must we be tested? How much longer must we die to live on our land? Will it never cease!"* He wept for those who would die or be maimed, for the families that would be forever broken, for the ignorance and cruelty of mankind; but most of all, he wept for himself, for having succumbed to anger and despair.

The following morning, David went to Jerusalem's regimental headquarters, located on Rehov Straus. The roads were empty as most of the city's residents were in bomb shelters. The only sounds that could be heard were the constant explosions. David was asked to escort a journalist with the Army Radio, named Ran Kochman, who carried a tape recorder, but did not know how to drive. Driving with him, Ran confided he had heard that Israel's Air Force had knocked out all of the Egyptian air force bases.

"Does that mean we're winning?" David asked.

"It means we have supremacy in the air," Ran explained, confidently.

David couldn't help but feel a sense of pride for Gideon, knowing he would have been part of that victory. "My friend, Gideon, is a pilot."

"So is my brother." As soon as he spoke of him, Ran shifted with unease.

The building on Rehov Straus was several stories tall. On the rooftop, men were observing the action overhead when David and Ran arrived. Ran began immediately tape recording a commentary of the events. All of Jerusalem was spread out below. Beyond the city, David could see Mount Scopus and the Mount of Olives. He watched as Israeli planes dived repeatedly on Jordanian positions, and could see tanks maneuvering on the ground.

Ran told him to look to the north, pointing out the destruction of King Hussein's unfinished palace and the police academy next to it. "If you look carefully to the south, you can see the fighting in Armon Hanatziv." David felt he was watching an epic war movie like the ones he had enjoyed as a boy, except this was the real thing and he was in a front row seat in the midst of it.

A few floors below, Ran used the abandoned switchboard to send his recordings to the radio studio in Jaffa. With vehicles in short supply, David was assigned to drive a blue 1953 Volkswagen to the battlefields surrounding Jerusalem so that Ran could cover as much of the action as possible.

Madame Aziza drove as fast as she could toward Jaffa Gate, with her ammunition of sandwiches, pastries and cold drinks and, just in case, her revolver. No longer willing to sit at home, or worse, in a shelter, she had volunteered like many other women who had cars to deliver provisions to the soldiers. The mission made her feel safer and, more importantly, useful.

The soldiers greeted her warmly, their eyes red and swollen with fatigue. She helped to replenish them with food, drinks and encouragement. Under normal circumstances, she viewed soldiers as potential clients; now, she treated them as if they were her own sons. These were her boys fighting for her life and everyone else's. She openly expressed her patriotic feelings and prayers for each one, feeling an essential part of the war effort.

At the edge of the eastern hills, where much of the heavy fighting was taking place, she stood encouraging and feeding all the soldiers she could reach. When an officer requested the use of her car to transport soldiers to join their platoon, she did not hesitate to give it to him. He took her name and address to assure her the car would be returned.

Among the army vehicles driving toward Jaffa Gate, she saw a dilapidated blue Volkswagen. As it got closer, she recognized one of the civilians inside.

"Good to see you, Mr. Englishman."

Feeling his face flush with embarrassment, David replied, cordially, "good to see you, too."

Not far from Jerusalem, across the Samarian Hills, Israeli fighter planes were striking Jordanian posts, giving cover to the soldiers who were entering Jalazon Village. The village was chiseled out of a stony hillside where Palestinian refugees were living under King Hussein's rule. When the first Israeli soldiers arrived at the village, the villagers mistook them for Jordanians and greeted them enthusiastically.

David and Ran, accompanied by two soldiers they had picked up, and Madame Aziza, who had insisted on joining them as she spoke Arabic and "would be indispensable as an interpreter," approached the village. It was in total chaos. Panicked families were fleeing, making the road impassable.

Ran and the soldiers took off with a passing platoon. David was asked by the commander to head back down the hill and pick up supplies for the troops. Madame Aziza's only way back was with him, but the main road had become blocked by refugees fleeing the village. She asked one of the refugees in Arabic if there was another road they could take. An elderly Palestinian pointed in the direction of a parallel road that he said joined up with the main road further down the mountain.

The road was covered in deep ruts and, in places, was obstructed by fallen rocks. Along the roadside were large scattered boulders and dry brush. David drove at a snail's pace, hoping the Volkswagen would not get stuck in a pothole or slip off the edge, but, soon after heading down the mountain, the car slid into a ditch and would not move.

Finding herself alone in a war zone with an unarmed British civilian, who was also a former client, and with their only means of escape stuck in a ditch, Madame Aziza became very anxious. Whenever she was nervous or fearful, her "bladder problem" became exacerbated and she had to urinate. She excused herself to search for somewhere to relieve herself. Seeking privacy, she walked down the hill to find a place where she would be shielded from view. David searched the trunk of the car for anything that might help get the car out of the ditch, but found nothing. Frustrated, he yelled every English curse word he knew as he attempted to push the car out. His shirt drenched in sweat, he rested his head on the car thinking how stupid he had been to take Madame Aziza's advice to follow the old Arab's direction. It not only put them both in danger, but forced him to be alone with her as well.

From the moment David had seen Madame Aziza at the Jaffa Gate, he had thought of Tamar. Yearning for her in the middle of this war was intolerable. How could he be possessed by desire when so many were being wounded and dying?

Out of nowhere, he heard "Do you need a hand?" as an unarmed soldier approached him, limping from an injury to his leg. He had strong features with a prominent cleft chin. David thought him his own age. He addressed David in English, offering to help push the car. He was slender, wearing a uniform that hung loosely on him. He spoke English with a British inflection and, by the manner in which he spoke, David knew he was well-educated.

The soldier introduced himself as Moshe and explained how, after his leg had been injured, he had become separated from his platoon. He was now trying to get back to Jerusalem. David was grateful for the offer of help. He felt he was a gift from heaven. After several strenuous attempts, David and Moshe managed to get the car back on the road. He offered to take the soldier to Hadassah Hospital for his injured leg, but he insisted, "It's not serious. I'll be fine. If you just give me a lift down the hill, I'll catch up with the others."

When Madame Aziza returned, she saw the young soldier standing with David and that the Volkswagen had been rescued from the ditch. David introduced Moshe and told her how fortunate it was that he had come along and helped push the car.

She studied the soldier, who stood frozen. David suddenly wondered if Moshe was one of her clients. She spoke rapidly in Hebrew to him. When he did not respond and avoided eye contact, she slapped him hard across the face, yelling at him in Arabic.

The soldier responded angrily in English, "I don't belong to Fatah or the PLO. I just want to get to Jerusalem."

"So you can try to kill more of us there!" Madame Aziza retorted in English.

"No! So I can return to England."

The soldier confessed that his real name was Omar Sadallah. He was Palestinian, a student at the London School of Economics on a scholarship, but, as a citizen of Jordan, he had been ordered home to join the army. His family, formerly from Jerusalem, was now living in Jalazon. Had he not agreed to return home, he would have brought shame and dishonor to them. He had never even held a gun, having been a student most of his life. As soon as he arrived in Jalazon, he had been thrust into the Jordanian army and had been wounded within the first hours of the war. Realizing it had been a mistake to come home, he had escaped from his unit and was using this obscure back road in an attempt to reach Jerusalem, where he had an uncle. When he heard David swearing in English and found the Volkswagen stuck in a ditch, he thought he had found salvation.

Madame Aziza thought it was "a good story." There was no way she would "trust anything an Arab said."

David believed Omar and felt compassion for his plight. "He's hurt and unarmed. There's no harm in him coming with us," David said.

"Are you crazy? He's the enemy!" She screamed.

This gentle, understanding and gracious woman had turned into a shrieking shrew. David looked at Omar and said, calmly, "I don't think he is." Trying to show the practical side of the situation, he added, "We may need his help again on this bloody road."

Madame Aziza, speaking in Arabic, pulled out her gun, aiming it at Omar's head.

"What are you doing?" David cried out in panic.

Omar calmly translated to David. "She just informed me, should I try to kill her, she would kill me first."

The Volkswagen, with Madame Aziza in the rear holding her gun, got stuck time and again in the endless potholes. Each time David and Omar pushed the car out, she complained bitterly about being "stuck on this dreadful road with the enemy and no end in sight." The drive was painfully slow. Madame Aziza made it worse with her anger toward the Arabs. "How stupid all Arabs were to trust that maniac Nasser. They are nothing more than donkeys who believe everything they are told," she insisted. "God must love those who are stupid because he makes so many of them."

Omar remained silent throughout her barrage of insults, focusing only on getting to his relatives in Jerusalem so he could escape back to England. David and Omar were drenched in sweat and their backs ached from the strenuous pushing. Exhausted, they rested on a large boulder, eating the remains of Madame Aziza's pastries and drinking warm sodas as Israeli planes roared overhead.

Resigned to the fact that she was dependent on both men to get her to safety, Madame Aziza listened as David and Omar talked about Omar's studies. David asked why he had chosen to study economics in England. He explained that he had won a scholarship to the London School of Economics. He had always felt that "economics was the power behind everything." David spoke of his studies at St. Andrew's in Scotland, where he had studied philosophy and literature, hoping to better understand the world.

Their conversation drifted to the war. David could not fathom why the Arabs viewed Israel with such hatred, after all "they are both Semites, who had lived in the region for millennia."

Omar looked at David, "Try living in the Jalazon Village as a refugee."

"You made your bed, now you don't like the way you sleep!?" Madame Aziza screamed.

David was sorry and felt stupid to bring up a subject that was painful for both of them. "Let's just keep our minds on getting back safely. It's best for all of us."

Omar felt the need to address David's question. "Besides taking our land ..."

"Your land?" Madame Aziza interjected.

"Israel is a threat to the Arab world," Omar said, flatly.

"Why?"

"It's a democracy, with its eyes on the future."

"Why is that a problem?"

"Most of the Arab world is poorly educated. They are taught to obey their leaders, not question them. They revere the past, not the future."

David asked Omar about his family in Jerusalem, why they remained there and his parents didn't.

"My father chose to leave, hoping to return when things became as before."

Madame Aziza gave out a big "Ha! Like most Arabs, he's praying for us to be killed. The acorn doesn't fall far from the tree."

Omar ignored her. He knew from his father, to argue is to lose the argument. Choosing to let her words fall on deaf ears, he continued his conversation with David. "My uncle stayed and still lives in the house I was born in. At least he and his family enjoy the conveniences of modern life, while we, as second-class citizens of Jordan, struggle to survive. My uncle's eldest son, Tabarik, became a doctor."

"Will he look after your leg, then?"

"Yes, of course."

Omar had not been able to talk freely since he returned home. Finding David sympathetic to his plight, he desired to reveal more about himself.

"As a boy, I would accompany my father to the mosque. The mullahs preached that our rewards would be in heaven. I chose to find my rewards in this world. I knew I had to move on."

David was astonished to hear Omar speak so unemotionally, as if he were an outsider, a man who had become alienated from his own culture. Despite her fear and prejudice, Madame Aziza found herself intrigued by Omar's unattached clarity.

David quoted Socrates, "A truly free individual is free only to the extent of his own self-mastery. The others are condemned to find masters to govern over them."

Omar acknowledged their shared philosophy with a smile. David felt a kinship with him. He wondered what he himself would have become had he grown up under Omar's circumstances.

Omar continued to speak. "Most Arabs believe women are sinful. They feel threatened by their power. An educated woman is believed to be more than dangerous. My wife, who is British, refuses to come with me when I visit my family, for fear of that mentality."

Madame Aziza wanted to know more about Omar's wife, but dared not ask, being unwilling to let go of her own judgment, pride and prejudice towards the Arabs. Although she now felt somewhat ashamed of her behavior toward Omar, she did not apologize.

"I've recently married and applied for British citizenship." Omar smiled like a child when he boasted about his wife, Margaret, who was studying for her doctorate in biology. "Other than myself, she believes Middle Eastern people are not cut out for life in a western society."

David found this theory amusing, thinking of his mother's own reference to "gracious living." He did not dare add that many of his English friends shared the same thoughts about Israelis, knowing Madame Aziza was listening carefully.

"It's true about the Arabs, not the Jews," Madame Aziza said, defiantly.

"What's it like being married to an English woman? Isn't there a culture clash?"

"Margaret is the only English woman I've ever really known. She was my English tutor when I arrived in London," Omar confessed. "Despite her prejudice, fate brought us together, and against all odds we fell in love."

"Is she much different from the women you've known here?" David asked.

Omar's eyes saddened, "Here, when women give birth, they are taught to nourish and nurture us. Then, they must give up their daughters to marriage, and their sons to war. Their reward as women is to be dismissed and grow dull and old before their time."

Madame Aziza looked at this young Arab's face when he spoke. She saw a vulnerability that comes from having known pain. So young and wise, she thought, and wondered how many more Arabs were like him.

They drove on quietly, sipping warm sodas when, in the near distance, the blast of a rocket sounded off. After a few anxious moments, Omar turned to David. "What brings an Englishman to a war that's not his?"

From the rear of the car, waiting for a response, David felt Madame Aziza's eyes on the back of his head.

"I came to help my cousin and friends." As soon as David heard those words he felt ashamed. He wondered what Omar would think if he knew he was there primarily because he had fallen in love with one of Madame Aziza's whores who he couldn't get out of his mind.

"You should be grateful for having had the good fortune to be born in England. As a Palestinian, I have had to learn to exist in a dual world to survive."

"I imagine that must be hard."

"The difficulty is when you must leave behind all that means so much to you, family, friends, the land you were born in and love."

The road was too narrow for David to avoid yet another lurch into the ditch. He and Omar once again pushed the car from behind while Madame Aziza, sitting behind the wheel, steered it out. Stressed from the endless ditches, she inadvertently shifted into reverse. Had they both not instinctively jumped away, she would have knocked them down. They pushed the car out with their last bit of strength, and continued driving cautiously, hoping the road ahead would prove to be less treacherous. Oblivious to the sounds of war all about them, Omar looked out at the hills as if it were the first and last time he would see them.

"Do you think when this war is over, there can be peace here?" David asked.

"There is too much fear and self-righteousness. The gap is too wide."

"Surely there must be a way to begin building a bridge," David argued.

"Not when people have no hope or nothing to lose but their lives. The Jews have everything to lose with just one war. Peace is in their best interest, not ours, and we know that," Omar said, coldly.

David felt chilled. Suddenly, the idea that Madame Aziza was right and that Omar would try to kill them before they reached Jerusalem unnerved him. It was only when he remembered Madame Aziza's gun that he was able to overcome his fear.

Madame Aziza broke into a fierce rage. "You see! Now that we helped him, he speaks like a real Arab! He believes like all the Arabs, in their blind stupidity, it's our fault they have no hope! When they wake up and find the courage to declare war on their real enemies, then they'll find hope!"

David feared Omar had had enough of her insults and would explode.

"This isn't helping to get us back."

Traveling in a seemingly endless, uncomfortable silence, David prayed there would be no more potholes when, up ahead, he finally saw the fork which connected them back onto the main road. Liberated from the ditches, David sped toward Jerusalem.

Jaffa Road was packed with army vehicles and soldiers. Driving through slowly, David looked into his rear-view mirror at Madame Aziza, fearful she would now turn Omar in.

Omar sat frozen, awaiting his fate. Knowing he was powerless to do anything, he glanced at David, then met Madame Aziza's eyes through the rearview mirror.

It was only when they reached the bottom of the road, that her decision to keep quiet became known.

David dropped Omar off down the hillside from the water mill, near the now vacant Jordanian sentry post. He shook his hand, wishing him a safe return home, and was embarrassed when Omar gave him a warm hug. In the midst of war, David had found and lost a kindred spirit. He watched him walk away, hoping the war would end soon and that Omar would be able to leave for England.

As much as Madame Aziza wanted to wish Omar well, she couldn't. After all, he was an Arab and life had long taught her that what Arabs said and what they did were two very different things. She also knew that, in taking the back road to Jerusalem, there had been no mistake, just the Hand of God revealing itself.

David drove Madame Aziza to Rehov Agripas. In their silence was a shared understanding of the fragility of each life.

Arriving at her house, David asked if there was a nearby shelter she could go to.

"No, and I have no intention of going to one either."

Before leaving, she turned to him, looked steadily into his eyes so that he would know she was telling the truth, and declared "you were the only client she ever had," before quickly vanishing into her house.

David worked through much of the night, catching just three hours sleep on a bed of blankets on the stone floor of the hospital's cafeteria. Obsessed with thoughts of Tamar, he did not know which was depleting him more, the war, or his desperate desire to find her. Madame Aziza's words echoed repeatedly in his mind. "You were the only client she ever had."

His body ached with fatigue. The black coffee no longer helped. As soon as this war ended, David swore, he would never drink another cup of that mud again.

In the early morning of Wednesday, June seventh, after dropping off two wounded soldiers at Hadassah Hospital, David headed for the King David Hotel to pick up Ran.

Ran now carried a walkie-talkie on which he could hear the field commanders. Driving up Jaffa Road, shouting barked out of it. Ran's eyes opened wide with disbelief. "What is it?" David demanded.

"That's Motti Gur's voice. He just ordered all battalion commanders to enter the Old City of Jerusalem."

Driving toward Lions Gate, they saw it was jammed by tanks with jubilant soldiers on top, entering the Old City. Ran told David to drive quickly to the Mandelbaum Gate, which had long served as a crossing point between Jewish and Arab Jerusalem. Leaving the Volkswagen outside the gate, they continued on foot, carrying only the tape recorder and a knapsack with its supplies. Paratroopers were rushing through this gate as well. Ran flashed their passes to the young officer and ran after the troopers through the gate and into the Old City. The area was still under sniper and artillery fire from the Mount of Olives.

Running just ahead of them was the chief rabbi of the Israeli army, General Shlomo Goren, carrying a shofar and a Bible. David, Ran and Goren were the only ones without helmets or weapons. They ran down dozens of steps, staying as close to the right wall of the Old City as they could. David felt his heart racing. Ran was out of breath but continued to describe into the microphone what was happening, hyperventilating and speaking in broken sentences. "We are following ... dozens of paratroopers and soldiers ... being led by Generals Haim Bar-Lev ...

and Uzi Narkiss ... as we enter the Old City."

Rabbi Goren, in a heightened state, began to blow his shofar. When they reached the Temple Mount, he blew his shofar even more rigorously. Then he began exuberantly reciting prayers. The religious soldiers placed their *kipahs* on their heads before joining the others praying at the Wailing Wall. Goren's excitement caught on and from every direction came cries of "Amen." After fighting for six continuous days, the soldiers, numb from exhaustion, with tears streaming down their grimy faces, burst into a chorus of "*Yerusallayim Shel Zahav,*" Jerusalem of Gold.

Ran could barely speak and his words crackled. "The war's over. We've won. Not since the Romans destroyed the temple has Jerusalem been united, or we Jews allowed to pray here."

Touching the Wall, David leaned his head against it, and found himself sobbing with emotions he did not understand or know he possessed.

The bleeding had stopped, but Sarah refused to leave her bed. She was determined to lie there, just as Esther had done, until she was assured there was no more danger of losing her child.

The shelling stopped for the first time in six days. Reb Eli returned from the shelter to the solitude of his study. Grateful for the quiet, he fell asleep, only to be awakened by loud shouting from the courtyard. He ran outside to see what all the noise was about.

People were crying out, "The war is over! It's over! We won! We won!" They repeated it over and over as if to make certain it was true.

Itzhak, an elderly recent widower who lived just across the way, pulled a radio to the window so all could hear. "Listen, listen!" he cried as the radio announced, "The war is over. Jerusalem has been reunited. Victory is ours." He turned up the radio so all could hear the singing of "Jerusalem of Gold."

From her bedroom window, Sarah stood watching women, children and men in the streets of Mea Shearim weeping copiously, embracing, holding onto each other in joyous awe and disbelief. Overcome with emotion, some fell to their knees in prayer, crying out, "A miracle, a miracle, thank you *Hashem* for saving us."

The rebbe looked up at Sarah's window where she stood weeping, and cried out in prayer, thankful for their deliverance, *"Baruch Atah Adonai Eloheinu Melech ha'olam, ha-gomel l'hayavim tovot sheg'malani kol tov."*

SEVEN

David stood with Anat, Ronit and Jonathan in the national cemetery on the slopes of Mount Herzl, as mourners gathered to honor one of their fallen heroes. Gideon had been killed on the first day of the war. Nilli held onto her inconsolable parents.

Assaf Halevi, a pilot and close friend of Gideon, was part of "Operation Moked" that destroyed three hundred Egyptian bombers, fighter planes and helicopters in less than two hours on the first day of the war, eliminating the main air threat to Israel.

He spoke of how twelve of their finest pilots had been killed, how Gideon had taken the most vulnerable position in the formation, knowing he would likely be the first to be shot down. Assaf's voice broke when he told how Gideon had taped the mezuzah his father had given him into his cockpit before setting out on the mission.

An air force commander who had lost his arm took over to speak. "The cost of the war has been immense. Seven hundred and seventy-seven soldiers are dead, and two thousand, five hundred and eighty-six have been wounded. Lieutenant Gideon Hurvitz exemplified the courage of our armed forces. We, along with all of our country, are in mourning." The commander saluted Gideon's coffin, then handed the folded flag to Gideon's mother.

Six jets flew overhead in the formation of the Star of David. Afterwards, they all flew low in salute of Gideon, then dispersed high into the sky where they disappeared, immortalizing him into infinity, at which moment his mother collapsed.

In celebration of victory, a military parade moved solemnly down Ben Yehuda Street. Spectators, overcome with gratitude, threw flowers and kissed the hands of passing soldiers. Instead of the eradication of Israel promised by Arab leaders, the Golan Heights, the Gaza Strip and the West Bank had been captured, more than tripling the territory under Israeli control.

Anat and David watched the spectacle from the third floor terrace of Anat's parents' flat on Ben Yehuda Street. Gideon's death hung over David, weighing him with an unshakable sadness. It had taken the loss of Gideon for him to realize how much their brief friendship had meant to him. Gideon had opened his heart to his ancestral home. Now Gideon, along with all the others who had fallen, belonged to its endless struggle and sacrifice.

Needing to get away from the parade and the oppressive crowds, Anat and David left for Abu Tor. Their loss followed them as they walked through the side streets. When they reached the windmill in Yermin Moshe, Anat pointed out how, "in just six days, Abu Tor has become the center of Jerusalem." Her thoughts still with Gideon she asked, "Have you heard from Jonathan?"

"He rang this morning. The whole kibbutz participated in the family's *shiva.*"

"It's so hard for people like the Hurwitzes. They're holocaust survivors. They lost two children and most of their family. I don't know if they have it left in them to deal with the death of another child."

"Gideon never mentioned that," David said, with numbed disbelief.

"Why would he?"

"I don't understand," David confessed. "I only know there is so much grief here, and now I'm part of it. Perhaps that's why people like my mother don't want to identify with being a Jew."

David's introspection angered Anat. "You can always join her in England."

Anat's words stung him. "I think I've passed the point of no return. I didn't mean to be insensitive or make you angry," David said, apologetically.

"I hate Jews like your mother, when so much of our blood has been spilled so she can live safely in England!" Anat let out a lurching sob, "I'm glad you're here and alive. I only wish Gideon and the others were too."

"So do I."

Walking up the hill of Abu Tor, they stood looking out at the Old City. "I know how many casualties there were in the Golan Heights. It must have been awful," David acknowledged, feeling how much she had witnessed. Her frivolous nature was nowhere to be found. At her parent's flat, he noticed she hardly ate the lunch her mother had prepared and seemed to drift off into her own thoughts.

Anat listened intently when he described his encounter with Madame Aziza and Omar. "Had we met under different circumstances, I would have liked to get to know him better."

"I'm glad you helped Omar. One less Arab to hate us."

He confided how guilty and ridiculous he felt thinking about Tamar throughout the war, how much it made his desire for her more intense.

She was as bewildered as he was by Madame Aziza's declaration that he had been Tamar's only client. "I don't believe she was telling the truth. It's her business to create fantasies."

"I believe her. There was no reason for her to lie to me."

They sat at the top of the hill on the stone wall surrounding Abu Tor watching the sun go down behind the Valley of Hinnon when Anat announced, in her prosaic manner, "I'm getting married."

David swung to face her and looked closely to see if she was joking.

"He is the colonel who was in command on the Golan," she said, seriously.

"This is a surprise. Had you known him before?" David inquired, not knowing how to digest this sudden development.

"No. We got to know each other very quickly. When you watch the dying and wounded, six days is an eternity," she said, fiercely.

"Ariel is strong. He's a fearless leader who was always in the front line with his men. This war taught me it's men like him who can show us the strength and courage we need to win, and how much a woman needs such a man to protect her."

"Do you love him?"

"I love his power."

"Is that enough?"

"For now, yes."

David wondered if all women felt like this. Was power so

important to them? Did they all need to feel protected?

As though she could read his mind, Anat said, "Perhaps in other parts of the world a woman's needs are different. Here, it's a matter of survival."

By the look in his eyes, Madame Aziza knew he wasn't going to leave without knowing the truth. "Tell me everything."

"She asked for you."

"What?"

"She asked for the 'Englishman' to be her only client."

Stunned, David repeated what she said to make sure he had heard correctly. "Specifically asked for me?"

"Yes. She asked for the Englishman," she said, but not telling him that Tamar never accepted any payment, that it was she alone who had benefited from all the money he had paid to be with her.

"I don't understand."

"Neither do I."

David sat bewildered. "Is there any way I can find her?"

"She came mysteriously and left the same way. I will let you know if I hear from her, but I don't think I will."

Reb Eli sat in stunned silence. He tried to collect his thoughts, but they had fallen into an abyss. Words failed to come forth. Paralyzed, he remained motionless, praying some wisdom would surface to guide him through his astonishment.

Sarah had promised herself that she would remain stoic when she confided her situation to her father. She knew how it would shock him and prayed her father's wise and understanding ways would prevail in helping her.

Now, sitting before him, she wept, stumbling for words to ask for his forgiveness. She saw the pain, humiliation and betrayal in her father's eyes.

"I never meant to shame you or bring shame on all of us. Please believe me. I could not imagine it would come to this. The love in my heart was a private matter, which I never meant or believed would bring dishonor to you."

"Who is the father?" the rebbe inquired.

"Please don't ask me. I cannot reveal his identity."

The rebbe felt his heart sink before he could speak. "Is he married?"

"No. And he is not from Mea Shearim. He is not an observant man," Sarah said, hoping to put an end to her father's inquiries.

Reb Eli held his head in bewilderment, wondering how Sarah could have met a man outside Mea Shearim where she lived, worked and seldom ventured from except to go to the market.

"Does this man love you as you love him?" he asked, cautiously.

"I don't believe so," Sarah confided, sadly.

"Does he know that you are carrying his child?"

"No, and I don't want him to know. Please respect my wishes," Sarah said, with all the strength she possessed.

All the rebbe was able to say was, "What are you going to do?"

"There is only one thing I can do. Leave and make a life for myself and my child."

"Where will you go?"

"I don't know, perhaps to America where I could continue to teach. No one would know who I am. I could say my husband died in the war."

"Is that what you want?" he asked, feeling his heart sinking.

Believing she had no other choice, Sarah said, "Yes, it's what I must do."

At times when his heart became heavy with burdens, Reb Eli would hear the voice of his grandfather, Reb Shlomo, saying, "*Whenever there is a fierce storm we must bend like a palm tree rather than be uprooted like a stiff, old oak.*"

The rebbe prayed and asked *Hashem* to guide him.Which way do I bend? This is my blood, my child who has no mother to comfort her. What do I do? Where do I send her, to strangers, to a foreign land, alone, carrying a child? Who will be there to help when she gives birth? Who will be there to help with the child? Everyone she loves and everyone who loves her are here. This is where she belongs.

How often he taught that our words must not differ from our thoughts; the inner and outer person must be the same; what is in the heart should be on the lips. But today, before his daughter, he had withheld his innermost feelings of betrayal and shock, knowing he was forbidden to deceive anyone, knowing he must honor all with integrity and a pure heart, for that is what is required of us all. Today, he had betrayed not only himself, but also his daughter.

His grandfather's voice began to bellow in his head, *"The elders teach us history and tradition. Our children teach us life."*

Madame Aziza placed the delicate tray before David, with offerings of tea spiced with rose water, and bite-sized biscuits filled with raspberries and almonds, accompanied by a perfect red rose. She spoke softly, once again resuming her role as the supreme enchantress with her charming ways and rituals. She felt a kinship with the Englishman, who had fallen into despair over the young woman who mystified her as much as him and it saddened her that she could not offer him any consolation.

"Women are like electricity. You don't have to know how it works to get a shock. The best part of a woman is in the discovery. It's what makes men's senses come alive," she said, hoping to dispel David's despair.

David found no comfort in her words and continued to probe for information she did not have. He even repeated questions in hope of finding a clue to Tamar's whereabouts.

"Have any of the other women requested to have only one client?" David asked, desperately trying to understand more.

Madame Aziza thought carefully, "Yes, a few requested certain ones once they became their regular clients. It was only Tamar who specifically asked for you."

David began to wonder if perhaps she was making all this up to flatter him. "How could she possibly ask for me, someone she didn't even know?"

"Are you sure you never knew her from before, perhaps in England?"

"Certainly, if I'd known or met Tamar in England, I would remember."

"I am as baffled as you are," was all she could offer.

On the other end of the phone, Reb Eli could hear the excitement and pride in Phillip Bennett's voice. Israel's victory was personal for him. He had helped raise millions for its defense and his reward was to be part of its victory. Now, as Phillip had done through the years, he was calling his old friend, inquiring how he and his family were doing and to see if there was anything he could do for him.

Reb Eli, as always, thanked him for his concern and assured him he was fine and in no need of anything. Phillip's commitment to Israel was all that was needed.

"Eli, are you sure there isn't something I could do for you?" Phillip asked, in the familiar, intimate tone established since their youth. "Surely you could use a bit of help Eli, everyone can at such times?"

"You have always been generous Phillip. It's been an honor to call you my friend. The truth is, you have been more than a brother to me."

"And you to me, Eli."

"Actually, there is something I could use a little help with, if it isn't too much of an imposition." The rebbe heard the words come forth before he knew what he was saying.

"Whatever it is, it would be my pleasure."

"It concerns my youngest daughter, Sarah."

Wandering alone in the early evening, through the narrow, stone-flagged alleyways of the Old City, David came across a large Arabic shingle hanging above an arched door. It included one English word, "Restaurant."

Earlier, he had walked through the Old City with Jonathan,

who had told him, "Since medieval times, the Old City had been divided into Jewish, Muslim, Christian and Armenian quarters, but its Jewish residents were expelled after the nineteen forty-eight Arab-Israel War. The Arabs then destroyed the entire Jewish quarter and did not allow Jews to enter the Old City." Today, its Arab residents waved white handkerchiefs of surrender from the windows above their shops. They cried out "Welcome, Shalom" to their curious victors who walked amongst them.

David's easy, intimate companionship with Jonathan had felt like old times. He hadn't realized how much he had missed it. Watching him walk out of the Jaffa Gate to join Nilli, he felt as if he were the only man left on earth. He knew Jonathan needed to support Nilli through her mourning. Her parents had found themselves unable to cope with the loss of Gideon and Jonathan was concerned that Nilli would become, "like many other children of holocaust survivors, the bearer of her parents' pain." He admonished himself for feeling upset by Jonathan's commitment to her.

He climbed the shabby stairs to the restaurant to find it was designed to resemble a tent fit for the sheiks of Arabia. The "tent" was draped in plush gold silk. Arabian tapestries covered the walls and the floor was covered with finely woven oriental carpets. Two men were seated on silk cushions surrounding a low brass-inlaid table which held a gas lantern. He could not make out if the men were Israelis or Arabs and suddenly wondered if he was in a place safe for Jews.

A middle-aged man with a thick, black mustache greeted him, "Shalom, welcome," he said, in a strong Arabic accent, inviting him to sit at one of the tables.

The menu was in Arabic and English, making it easy for David to order the salads, hummus and tehina he was familiar with from Mickey's. When they arrived, they proved to be superior.

When David heard the two men across the room conversing in Hebrew, he became more at ease. He was not adept at telling the difference between Arabs and Israelis, until they spoke. They looked the same to him. It was easy to have mistaken Omar for an Israeli.

David thought of the madness that prevailed in this part of the world. Just weeks ago, everyone was at war. Now, business took precedence. The person who hated you as a perceived enemy one minute could graciously serve you food in the next.

Finishing his tea, David paid the mustachioed man. Remembering Anat's words, "one less Arab to hate us," he felt inspired to leave a generous tip.

Outside, the air had cooled with the onset of night. To put off returning to his flat, he decided to walk through the alley, empty now that the shops had closed, and found himself in a long alleyway called "Via Dolorosa." He walked until he came to a courtyard with a small church. Inscribed on its arch was "IV Station of The Way of The Cross, Armenian Church."

Resting on the church steps, his thoughts drifted to Gideon and Nilli. He wept for Gideon and grieved for all the lives that had been lost, for all those scarred forever, and for the loss of the woman who had touched his heart and made him feel grateful to be alive. He sat cradling his head in his arms.

A stillness came upon him, accompanied by a sweet, soothing scent. His breathing slowed as the scent enveloped him, and he felt relaxed for the first time since the war. He was surprised to see a beggar in a tattered white robe resting on the steps to his left. The beggar lifted his head and gazed directly at him. David felt an immediate connection. He reached into his pocket and gave him all the money he had on him. The man nodded in thanks, and said quietly, "When you fall, remember, it's just another step towards elevation."

The church doors creaked open. David watched as two Armenian priests in black robes came down the steps and made their way through the courtyard. He turned back to the beggar, but he was gone.

EIGHT

Arriving in the serene beauty of the Hampshire countryside, Sarah was taken in by the quiet presence of its rolling hills and vast green, meandering meadows. Her familiar world seemed far away. She had been anxious about leaving the only home she had known to live in a foreign land with a woman she had never met.

Phillip Bennett had greeted her at London's Heathrow airport. His urbane, self-assured manner had inadvertently made her feel like a displaced refugee. It was only when he delivered her to his sister, Eleanor Wilding, that she began to feel genuinely welcomed. Eleanor's warm smile, soft-spoken voice and kind words, embraced and comforted her. She was as gracious and gentle as the countryside itself. She asked no questions of Sarah, other than making sure she was comfortable and had everything she needed. Sarah was enchanted by the charm of her seventeenth-century house, with its gables, thick mullioned windows, and huge fireplaces. Its grandness overwhelmed her. She had never imagined anyone could live like this, still less with servants. She was given her own private quarters with a large bathroom and study and invited to make herself at home in all of the house.

The stately home was quietly elegant and warm. Fine art and furnishings, with vintage Aubusson carpets on the dark wooden floors, reflected a timeless, pleasurable world. The house smelled of lavender and rose. Beautifully arranged orchids, mixed with roses gathered from the garden, were displayed everywhere. Stone fireplaces stood in the parlor, dining room and the conservatory, as well as in Sarah's bedroom. The conservatory and gardens delighted her most. She imagined within each flower were the sacred secrets of the universe.

Sleeping under the delicate, floral canopy of her bed, Sarah felt like a displaced person pretending to be a princess. She was grateful to *Hashem* for having been invited to live in such a home until her child was safely born.

Before arriving in England, she had anxiously mulled over her fears of running into David. Living in the countryside, she now knew all of her anxiety had been unfounded. She was certain that David lived in London, where surely he had gotten on with his life and forgotten the whore Tamar.

Eleanor had first met Sarah when she visited Eli shortly after her husband had been killed. She was a shy little girl with a head full of red hair and light hazel eyes that seemed to hold more wisdom than she had ever seen in a child. Eleanor remembered Eli's generosity and kindness after her husband's tragic accident, how his wisdom gently guided her through her pain, a pain she never believed would vanish from her heart. She remembered his promise, "With time your pain will become like the waves in the ocean, coming and going until all that remains is the gentle reminder of loving memories that will soothe your heart like a sacred prayer shawl." Sixteen years later, Eli's prophetic words had proven true.

In the solitude of her study, Eleanor sipped a glass of sherry, remembering when the *Kindertransport* had brought Eli to her childhood home. Four years younger than her brother and Eli, she had felt thwarted when the two boys developed a strong friendship that excluded her. Of all the children the Bennetts had taken into their home, Eli was the oldest and, therefore, the most difficult to place with a foster family. Given Eli's quiet, reserved manner, and the close bond that had developed between the two boys, Eleanor's parents had decided to keep Eli with them.

Although they lived under the same roof, Eleanor had had to watch from a distance as Eli began to grow into a deeply religious young man whose passion for Judaism she could not understand. She became enamored of his quiet intelligence and sensitivity. She could not help feeling jealous of Phillip and Eli's close relationship. She found Eli's preference for solitude annoyingly aloof, yet mysterious and intriguing. As attractive and bright as she was, all her clever attempts to get his attention failed, and she could not penetrate Eli's world.

Unbeknownst to anyone else in the household, she had grown to love Eli, knowing full well that neither he nor her family would ever accept the vast religious and social oceans that lay between them. Several years earlier, when news had come of Eli's nomination as Chief Rabbi of Jerusalem, she had felt great pride for the man who would remain her first and lasting love. When Eli was widowed several years after her husband had died, she wept for him.

The decision of her only child to live in Jerusalem and study Judaism had been met with shock, apprehension and embarrassment by the Bennetts. It was Eli who had welcomed Jonathan with open arms, just as he had done recently for David, her beloved nephew, who could not find his way in the world.

Eleanor felt privileged to be asked by Phillip and Eli to look after Sarah and promised to watch over her as if she were her own daughter. Phillip had told her of Sarah's pregnancy, the details of which Eli had not shared. They both knew Sarah had been left a young widow and concluded the father of her child must have perished in the Six Day War. They felt great compassion for her circumstances, given the religious community she lived in.

Sarah brought with her the same calm and sense of wellbeing her father carried. Eleanor delighted in the peaceful presence that relieved the loneliness of her empty house. Sarah was gracious and considerate, never assuming anything, grateful for the slightest kindness shown her. Eleanor felt saddened by the thought that such a beautiful young woman should be left to carry the burden of raising a child on her own, with no resources but a teaching position in an orthodox school. Her sister-in-law, Victoria, had warned, "She'll most likely arrive wearing an awful wig and a dreary orthodox outfit that will bring attention to her everywhere she goes." She was wrong. Sarah's lovely auburn hair flowed freely and her attire was simple, in modest good taste.

Eleanor felt pleased with herself for having made her kitchen kosher, knowing Reb Eli's daughter would be uncomfortable eating under any other circumstances. She informed her cook, Katie, about the transition and "new dietary laws." Katie was baffled and balked at needing to shop in London's "Jewish District," having never known, in over twenty years, that Eleanor Wilding was a Jew.

Invited by Prime Minister Levi Eshkol to offer prayers for the country, the Chief Rabbi of Jerusalem, Eliezer Ben-Jaacov, stood humbly before the Knesset, looking out at the faces that governed the land. He spoke with a prayer in his heart that they would hear the words of a higher power and be given the wisdom to guide the nation into a lasting peace with its neighbors.

> We are a people intimate with suffering. Let us pray first for those who have suffered most. If you feel blessed with victory in this war, I beg you, ask a mother who lost her son how victorious she feels.

Reb Eli's words echoed in the room and weighed heavily on everyone there. They had all lost a loved one, or knew someone who had.

> For the memory of all those we have lost, let us use our victory and strength to pursue peace with our neighbors. May we remember, victory brings relief, not triumph. Let us not fall into arrogance, for the Talmud teaches that "arrogance is a crown without a kingdom." Far greater than destroying our chance for peace, it will destroy our integrity, our humanity, our very souls.

> May we always remember, we are a nation governed by the laws of *Hashem* and the teachings of the Torah. God forbid we become so wearied by wars that we forget we are all one under God. The troubles of the world come from our failure to see His grandeur. When the

knowledge of God runs dry, we suffer, for we see the world, not as it is, but as who we are. And who are we? If I am not for myself, who will be for me? If I am not for others, what am I? And if not now, when?

Peace is the only way our children and our children's children can flourish in our land. With peace, we will know true victory. May we be blessed with the wisdom to create a righteous peace, and may God reveal His Torah to us all. May He who makes peace on high make peace on us and all of Israel and on all of the world"

Amen.

The rebbe closed his eyes in a moment of silent prayer. When he opened them, he saw the eyes of Yitzhak Rabin, the Chief of Staff, and Moshe Dayan, the Defense Minister, looking deeply into his. Reb Eli prayed, *Please God, that they heard me with their hearts.*

The heat in July was stifling as David walked up Ben Yeduda Street toward Mea Shearim. The hot *khamsin* winds brought with it locusts, flies and beetles larger than any he had ever seen. The stones of Jerusalem were baking in the sun.

"This is not like Jerusalem weather. I can't remember it being so hot. It's already 4:30, and still no relief," grumbled a perspiring pedestrian.

As oppressive as the heat was, David rushed through the courtyard to Reb Eli's house. He had not met with him since before the war. He felt his world had turned upside down and he needed shelter from the storm.

A standing fan circulated the hot air in the rebbe's study, providing little relief. The rebbe, as always, listened intently, his magnetic blue eyes never wandering as David told him about his encounter with Madame Aziza and Omar, what she had revealed about Tamar, and how frustrated and anguished he felt at not being able to find her. He confessed his guilt about not fighting during the war, his deep sadness at the loss of Gideon, and how much he now realized what Gideon's friendship had meant to him.

Reb Eli asked him what he had learned from all of this.

With the innocence of a child, David revealed how desperately lonely he had felt when Jonathan left him on his own to wander in the Old City. He realized it was the same, familiar loneliness he had lived with all his life, a feeling of being a foreigner in the world. The war had left him raw and even more conflicted about who he was and where he belonged.

David then described the incident at the Armenian Church. "Sitting there on the steps, I felt such despair, but then became suddenly peaceful. There was a lovely scent in the air. I noticed a beggar who said something to me, then disappeared when two priests distracted me. I've been unable to get him out of my mind."

"What did he say?"

"It was a bit cryptic. 'When you fall, remember, it's just another step towards elevation'."

Reb Eli leaned in closer. "Perhaps you had a visitation. It is said that the Prophet Elijah appears when people are in great distress. At times he is known to appear as a beggar."

"I don't believe in prophets. There must be a rational explanation for this."

"Do you know the significance of the Via Dolorosa?"

"No, I just remember seeing the name while walking. Why? Does it have some Jewish significance?"

"It's where Jesus was known to have walked on his final day. You were at a place of holiness and great suffering."

He knew by the look on Jonathan's face that he should not have told him about his encounter at the Armenian Church.

"You need help, David. I know someone who is a specialist in the 'Jerusalem Syndrome.' It's a known phenomenon here. You've got to let me help you," Jonathan pleaded.

"Everyone suffering from the syndrome sees a biblical figure in the most likely places. In most cases, they're Christians who see Jesus or the apostles. Jews usually see Moses or King David; Muslims see Mohammed, although he never set foot in Jerusalem."

"I'm sorry I shared this with you. It never occurred to me you would mistake a profound, personal experience for madness."

"David, since you've been here, you've fallen in love with a prostitute, aided an enemy during the war, and spoken with an imaginary prophet on the Via Dolorosa! " Jonathan retorted, losing his patience.

"I'm sorry. I won't be bothering you with this any more."

"Oh come off it! Stop pouting like a child. After six days of hell, we're alive when so many others have died or been wounded. Isn't that enough of a miracle?"

Exploding with all his pain and anger, David cried out, "I'm not looking for miracles. I want to know where I belong in all of this! The only thing I know is what I see, hear, think and feel. It's all I know."

"It's all any of us know, until we find a spiritual path," Jonathan said, calmly.

"Yes, and you have found yours in Judaism. I still need to find mine."

"I hope you do, David. I hope you do."

After weeks of continuous rain, the sunny day was a welcome relief. Eleanor could hear Sarah chanting her prayers, a ritual she practiced every morning and evening. Waiting for her at the breakfast table, she was concerned about Sarah's attempts to hide her loneliness with cordiality and her ready smile. She was always eager to please, but her sad, longing eyes betrayed her.

In nearby Winchester, a historic city that had once served as the capital of England and a haven for Jews, Sarah was disappointed to learn that the synagogue was long gone. "Jewry Street" remained the only reminder of the community's once prominent presence.

She reveled in the city's history, reading everything she could find about its cathedral, ancient ruins and gardens. Walking along the river Itchen, she stood still, mesmerized by the flow of its rushing water. When it was time for lunch, she pleaded childishly to eat within sight of the river, to which Eleanor gladly agreed.

Sitting by the window in the turret of a café on the riverbank, the sadness lurked in Sarah's eyes. Eleanor wished she could reach out and comfort her, knowing how much a young woman needed the comfort of a mother's touch when she was having a child, especially without a husband. Her fondness for the girl had grown deeper and stronger, day-by-day. In an attempt to dispel her sadness, Eleanor continued with bright conversation about the city and how lovely it was to have such a warm, sunny day.

Sarah's eyes kept watch on the river.

Eleanor noticed she had not eaten much of her pasta and asked, "Was the food all right?"

"It was very tasty, thank you."

Eleanor asked if there was anything else she wanted. "Perhaps a lovely, decadent dessert?"

"No, thank you."

"Sarah, is there anything you wish for that I can help you with?" Eleanor asked, gently.

"If I could learn to become like a river, and keep flowing with whatever comes before me," Sarah spoke simply, leaving Eleanor deeply affected.

Sarah's morning sickness continued. The nausea was so intense she could not eat a morsel of food until late afternoon. Eleanor had peppermint tea and salted tea biscuits prepared for her. When the nausea finally ceased, Sarah could see the soft, round bump of her pregnancy and delighted in feeling David's and her child growing inside her.

Eleanor suggested a trip to London. Sarah was immediately apprehensive, imagining what disaster would unfold if they ran into David on the streets of the city. She tortured herself with all sorts of dreadful possibilities, obsessing about what she could do to avoid them. Feigning illness was the simplest plan. She decided to dress in her orthodox garb and, if the need arose, feign illness and escape to "the ladies' parlor," as Eleanor liked to call it.

Eleanor arranged for them to be chauffeured to London. Gazing from the car window, she enjoyed the beauty of southern England, with its gentle, green hills divided by ancient hedgerows, the fields and farms looking as if they had been there since time began. As beautiful and peaceful as it was, the scenery did not quell the yearning for her family and her own country. Mostly, she longed for her father. A man of few words, she missed his presence, the smiling, knowing eyes, his kindness and prophetic wisdom. She hoped that, perhaps, London would distract her from the loneliness she felt.

The streets of the city excited and overwhelmed her at the same time. Women were stylishly dressed in miniskirts and high-heeled shoes, with matching colored leather handbags, their makeup just as dramatic as Madame Aziza's ladies. She could smell the faint scent of fine perfumes as women passed by. She noticed the confidence with which they carried themselves.

The bustle of the city and the grand scale of its architecture were so different from Tel Aviv, the only other big city she knew. Tel Aviv seemed so provincial in comparison. Struck by the contrast, she became poignantly aware of her position as an unmarried, orthodox Jewess, pregnant in a foreign land, estranged and invisible to all but Eleanor.

The walk through Hyde Park was a relief from the crowded streets and noise. Eleanor suggested they go to the restaurant overlooking the Serpentine for afternoon tea. Looking out at the lake, Sarah saw a young couple in a rowboat, kissing, oblivious to all but each other. Her heart sank when she imagined the man could be David. When tea and cheese sandwiches arrived, she quietly said her blessing before she bit into her sandwich, hoping it would alleviate the deep longing inside her.

"How are you feeling?" Eleanor asked, kindly.

"I'm fine, thank you," she said, in a pretense of cheerfulness.

"Thank goodness your morning sickness is over," Eleanor whispered. "Would you like to do some more sightseeing before we return home?"

"Eleanor, are you sure this isn't boring for you?"

"Don't be silly, I don't get the opportunity to enjoy London much. I'm grateful to be able to share it with you."

"Are you sure?"

"Yes, Sarah, I'm sure," Eleanor replied, ashamed of her embarrassment at Sarah's orthodox garb and her very public ritual prayer before eating. She so reminded her of Eli when he was her age. Her devotion to prayer, her quiet intelligence, her openness to learning, and, most importantly for Eleanor, the gentleness and serenity she brought to everything and everyone she encountered, so much like her father.

Along the River Thames, Eleanor pointed out Waterloo Bridge and the Houses of Parliament. Sarah had read up on all the historical places and knew their history. She remarked how it had been bombed during World War II, then rebuilt; how England had suffered during the blitz, resisting a German invasion.

"You know our history as well as we do," Eleanor said, admiring Sarah's intense interest and ability to learn quickly.

"I love learning about things that are foreign and unavailable to me."

The remark saddened Eleanor. She felt a sudden pang of guilt that such a bright, intelligent and inquisitive young woman should not have been as privileged and exposed to the knowledge of the world as she had, simply because of her religious confinement and economic status. She quickly pushed the thought aside. After all, there was so much injustice in the world, and not a lot she could do about it.

In Westminster Abbey, Sarah sat silently, in awe of its magnificence, as visitors quietly roamed about. Gazing at the soaring architecture, the statues and stained glass windows, she sat transfixed, absorbing every detail.

Outside, in the Abbey's courtyard, she remarked, "How magnificent to see God's creative force through the hands and imagination of men. The walls hold the joy and cries of their souls."

Before leaving London, they drove to Rutland Gardens in Knightsbridge to visit the Westminster Synagogue, which Sarah had asked to see. At the entrance to the street they found a gate with a small guardhouse. A uniformed guard nodded politely when they passed him. They walked several times up and down the street in search of the synagogue, returning to the guardhouse to inquire where it was.

The guard pointed to the corner house. "That's it, right there, the Kent House."

The synagogue bore no Jewish symbols other than a small, simple mezuzah discreetly nailed to the right side of the door-frame. Otherwise, the building was just like the rest of the handsome houses in the terrace.

Discovering the doors were locked, Eleanor rang the bell. A woman's voice came across the intercom inquiring who was there and what they wanted.

"Good afternoon, this is Lady Eleanor Wilding. I'm here with a friend from Jerusalem. May we visit your sanctuary?" There was a long pause before she answered.

"Please go to the delivery door to your right. I'll meet you there."

As they stood beside it, a stocky woman appeared.

"I'm sorry, the sanctuary is closed. Since the Six Day War, we have had to increase our security. The sanctuary can only be seen by appointment," she said.

Driving back to Hampshire, Sarah was glad her fears had been unfounded and she had not run into David. Instead, she had experienced what it felt like to be a Jew in a Christian world and she longed to be home among her own. She longed for her own language, her own culture, for Shabbat meals with singing children, candlelit prayers, the welcoming of the *shechinah.* She heard her father's words echo in her mind. "Even if you uproot a tree, it will miss its natural soil and falter." She yearned to walk on her own soil, that which nourished her soul.

Eleanor wondered if perhaps taking Sarah to London had been a mistake. She appeared to have withdrawn. She barely spoke unless asked a question and kept mostly to herself.

It was exactly as Eli would do when he was young, living in England and longing for home. How much she was made from the same fabric as her father.

To help ease her longing, Eleanor arranged a Shabbat dinner. The dining table was set with fine linen. Delft dinnerware and long-stemmed crystal wine glasses adorned the large oblong table. An elaborate, silver Shabbat Menorah from Jerusalem sat handsomely in the center of the table. The *challah* that Jessie had learned to bake to avoid the trip to London was covered with a gold-tasseled, satin-embroidered cloth. It pleased Eleanor to see Sarah's eyes gleam with pleasure when she saw how beautiful the dining hall had been arranged for Shabbat.

The only Jews Eleanor knew to invite were her brother, Phillip, and his wife, Victoria. The rest of the family lived in London, and, if they were to receive an invitation to a Shabbat dinner, they would fear she had gone religious, which was exactly the same as going mad as far as they were concerned.

Phillip and Victoria arrived. Victoria's diamond and sapphire earrings and necklace gave her a regal appearance. Phillip introduced his wife to Sarah, who wore a modest white blouse with a dark blue pleated skirt and a small, gold *Chai* around her neck, the only jewelry she possessed.

Before arriving at Eleanor's, Phillip had carefully coached his wife to be gentle in manner as Sarah was not only his dear friend's daughter, but also a sensitive, orthodox young woman in a precarious situation.

He repeated how delighted he was to be invited to celebrate a real Shabbat dinner. Victoria smiled graciously, insinuating that she shared the same sentiments, although she appeared ill-at-ease sitting at the table, especially when Phillip donned a *kipah* before Sarah recited the Sabbath blessings.

Eleanor knew how difficult it was for Victoria to attend this dinner. Jonathan's departure to study Judaism in Jerusalem had really worried her. She was concerned that word would get out and bring unwanted attention to the family. David's decision to visit him in Israel had been acceptable to her, given his wanderlust, but when he returned to Israel during the war, Victoria had become alarmed.

Like Eleanor, she came from a long line of wealthy Jewish families living in England. They had lived there since escaping from Spain during the Inquisition. Her family, the Abadias, became importers of precious stones and soon created a great amount of wealth. For business purposes, like many who escaped the Inquisition, the Abadias changed their Sephardic names to more anglicized ones. They became the "Andrews" family, owners of England's most prestigious jewelry business, catering not only to the wealthy, but to the royal family as well. They worked hard to assimilate and had been accepted into England's aristocracy. Most of their acquaintances belonged to the Church of England, where religious rituals other than their own were viewed in the same light as poor taste.

Jonathan's announcement of his decision to study in Jerusalem had been a shock to the family. He had never shown any religious aspirations or interest in Judaism. Eleanor knew Victoria secretly hoped he would stay in Israel, should he become religious, to avoid embarrassment for them all.

David's return to Israel had deeply disturbed Victoria. She realized it was not just another of his adventures and worried that her son had become "too involved." Eleanor knew this Shabbat dinner, being a Jewish ritual, would amplify Victoria's fears. Should it become a matter of routine, it would be a great cause of discomfort to her, which Eleanor could not help but secretly enjoy.

Dinner became uncomfortably quiet, inspiring Eleanor to tell of her outing to London with Sarah and how impressed she was with Sarah's knowledge of its history. Given her enthusiastic desire for knowledge and her teaching credentials, Phillip asked Sarah if perhaps she might be interested in a teaching position at an orthodox girls' school in London. He offered to help her find a job in one, should she want to remain in England.

Victoria thought it was a splendid idea. With Sarah's good looks, she was sure she would also find a suitable orthodox husband in England.

Victoria's tone and insensitivity and the suggestion of being with a another man caused Sarah to feel sick. She took small bites of her challah, hoping it would calm the discomfort in her stomach. Then suddenly, without having time to excuse herself, she rushed to the toilet to throw up. After rinsing her mouth and face with cold water, she returned to the table, composed.

"Is everything all right?" Eleanor asked, concerned.

"I'm fine, thank you," Sarah said, hoping the evening would end soon.

The Bennetts felt it best to ignore the incident and continued to eat and sip their wine, complementing Eleanor on a delicious meal.

Just as at each *Shabbat* evening at home, Sarah began to sing softly the closing *Shabbat* prayer. Tears began to sting. She closed her eyes, yearning to be home, yearning to be once more with David.

NINE

The letter tugged at Reb Eli's heart. It was not so much what Sarah had written, as what she had requested that so affected him. She had asked him to send her a small stone from Jerusalem, "Perhaps one that came from the *Kotel,*" promising to return it when she came home. He admonished himself for not recognizing the depth of her despair. What had it come to, for her to plead for a stone?

He struggled to pay attention to David as he spoke of his seductress, Tamar, and the anguish her loss was causing him. The rebbe's thoughts were now constantly with his daughter in exile.

David sensed there was something amiss with Reb Eli. In the past few weeks, he had seemed preoccupied. He missed having his full attention. He desperately needed the rebbe's guidance to help him cope with the vicious circle he found himself in. The more he tried to dismiss his longing for Tamar, the stronger it became.

David cautiously asked the rebbe, "Is there anything wrong? Is there any way I can be of help?"

Reb Eli apologized for his distraction and thanked David for his concern. "It's a complicated family matter, something I should have been more aware of and given more attention to."

David wondered what family situation could be so complicated it would cause Reb Eli such distress. Everyone, it seemed, had their own problems.

"Perhaps the burdens are what keep us reaching out to each other?" Reb Eli said, as much to himself as to David.

The rebbe had an hour before evening prayers. He didn't know what to do with his thoughts about Sarah. He went for a walk to clear his mind. Watching people as they passed by, he wondered what other fathers would do, given his daughter's predicament. His family insisted on knowing why she had gone abroad and when she was coming home. Mostly it was Miriam who besieged him with questions. The rebbe sighed, knowing there was no one to whom he, the chief rabbi of Jerusalem, the wise consoler of many, could turn. His daughter's exile from her family and community had taught him the full meaning of desolation, which he could share only with God.

Anat's new husband, Colonel Ariel Shemtov, was a tall, imposing man with eyes that seemed to see right through you. He was a career soldier who had fought in the War of Independence, the Suez War, and in continuous combat operations to contain insurgents from Egypt, Syria, and Jordan. He was sixteen years Anat's senior, and just as opinionated.

They lived in one of the old stone houses in Abu Tor, just down the road from David's flat. David listened as Ariel told him what Israel's national strategy should be. Unlike Anat, he spoke with a heavy Israeli accent. As Ariel smoked cigarettes and sipped Turkish coffee, David was disquieted by his relentless gaze.

"Israel faces the eternal problem of the Jews," Ariel insisted. "Jews think if only they can get the world to like them, they'll be safe. When did that ever work? And now that we've won a war with the entire Arab world, we are expected to apologize for surviving, and give back territory vital to our security? It was a mistake not to have taken Cairo. Nasser would have been brought to his knees. We could have forced a real peace."

"David, have you forgotten their promise to annihilate us, how we would be swimming with the fishes? Do you think the Arabs would have returned any of our land if they had won?" Anat demanded.

"Yes, but how will Israel deal with the Arabs in the conquered land?" David asked.

"We must make sure our borders are secure. The rest is their problem," Ariel replied.

"Perhaps there's now an opening for a new relationship with them? Surely, that would be to everyone's advantage," David argued.

"The Arabs will never accept us, not in our lifetime. They live in the Dark Ages. Their rulers want to keep them there. They teach them they are miserable because of us, not because of their policies. We serve as their boogey man. They can't afford to give us up. Everything we want, they don't. We believe in freedom and progress and look forward to a future where we can become innovators in every field. They cling to the past, to their fundamentalism," Ariel argued.

When David wondered aloud if Ariel's attitude would best serve Israel's future, Anat jumped in, "Now, because they lost the war that they started, they have a big refugee problem. Why should the burden be on us? Why don't they ask their hero, Nasser, what to do? Other countries dictate the peace terms when they win. Why should it be different for us? Why must we litigate, beg and give everything away in the hope of peace? We Jews are expected to be the only real Christians in the world. We are supposed to follow rules that exist only for us. If Nasser and the Arabs had won, they would have wiped us off the map, and no one would have lifted a finger to save us?"

"That's the point," David exclaimed. "There has to be a better solution. If Israel relies solely on its military, just one defeat can mean the end of the country."

"We've been hearing that from the political left for years. They live in a dream world where the good always overcomes. That is, until they are threatened with extinction. The orthodox are the same, only with them, they think God is on their side and is going to save them. He did a great job in the Holocaust! When they come to their senses, they look to us to save them," Ariel continued. "What they don't realize is that the Russian bastards are behind the Arabs' wars. They want a stronghold in the Middle East. They are as clever as the Arabs are stupid. And when you are stupid, you become a puppet."

"Israel now has the Sinai, the West Bank, the Golan Heights and all of Jerusalem. It has more than doubled in size. Surely there is a peace to be made in exchange for returning the land. If you can't make peace now, when will you?" David said, knowing there had to be more Arabs like Omar, who did not fit Ariel's stereotype.

"Agreements with the Arabs aren't worth the paper they are written on. This war was proof of that," Ariel said, emphatically.

Anat jumped in. "You just don't get it. The world does not treat us like other nations. If Israel goes, so will go all the Jews, and another Holocaust will be upon us. What worries me, David, is how you can be so oblivious to history. What more evidence do you need?"

David did not want to be judged ignorant for not agreeing with them. He knew the history. He believed people, including Jews and Arabs, could find a way to live together peacefully.

"I understand why it's easy for you to be a high-minded liberal. You can return to England and live as an incognito Jew and hide behind the shield of your family's status," she said.

David repressed his anger. "Frankly, I do realize that. It saddens me. But being a 'high-minded liberal' takes its own form of courage. I have to believe there's hope for us all to live in peace. Surely there are Arabs who are just like me."

"When you find them, let us know," Ariel said quietly, his gaze steadfast.

November was cold and dreary with seemingly endless rain. Sarah filled the days waiting for her child to be born with reading, prayer and intimate conversations with Eleanor. The weather kept them close to home, where they spent a great deal of time together. Their relationship had blossomed into the simple intimacy often shared between mothers and daughters. When Sarah could feel her baby's tiny feet kicking during afternoon tea, Eleanor would share in the delight. They enjoyed exploring the possible names it could be called. Should it be a girl, according to tradition Sarah would name her after her deceased mother, Hannah. She was not quite sure about a boy's name, as her father was still alive. Should it be a boy, she would decide on a name after the birth. In keeping with the laws of her religious belief, Sarah refused to prepare or allow Eleanor to buy anything for the baby until after it was born.

Sarah had not seen Victoria Bennett since that difficult Shabbat dinner months ago, and any thought or mention of her disturbed her. She had not seen much of Phillip Bennett either, other than during a few brief visits when he inquired politely about how she was feeling, and whether there was anything she needed.

Eleanor always felt gloomy through the winter months in Hampshire. In the past, she had enjoyed winter retreats to Spain and Portugal, but they had lost their appeal to her. Ever since her husband had died and Jonathan had left for Israel, wherever she went to escape her loneliness just seemed to intensify it. Eli's daughter brought warmth and joy to her home. Sarah was intelligent and mature for her years and her curiosity and open-mindedness delighted Eleanor.

When she noticed her discomfort at being served by the staff, Eleanor had Katie leave meals and tea on the sideboard, where she and Sarah could help themselves. Sarah insisted on helping to wash the produce and would clear the table before Katie could. She treated and spoke to her and the entire household in the same manner as she behaved toward Eleanor. Reb Eli's daughter knew no other way. Human kindness and *mitzvot* were how she understood to serve God.

There was only one door that Sarah kept closed, and that was any talk about the father of her child. Whenever Eleanor attempted to broach the subject, Sarah quietly withdrew and then talked about something else. Eleanor imagined that she must have loved him deeply and, having lost him to the war, must still be devastated. Eleanor watched her household transform from a well-managed and dutiful place into a high-spirited home, with everyone doing what they could to be pleasing, especially to Sarah. If she showed a craving for baked apple Danishes or raspberry scones, Katie made certain they were available every day. Sarah's delight in picking wildflowers on the estate encouraged Katie to mix them into the arrangements of orchids from the greenhouse.

Shabbat was now a regular household event: *challah* was baked, *kashrut* laws were abided by, and fowl was prepared with plums and apricots. Friday nights at dusk, Eleanor found herself looking forward to Sarah's lighting of the candles, welcoming the *shechinah*, with her beautiful singing. She reflected her father's love of Torah like a bright shining star bringing light, joy and loving kindness into Eleanor's life, as Eli had done before her.

Archaeologists were eager to excavate newly-accessible locations in the Old City. Projects at biblical sites came under the control of the *Rabbanute*, a bench of three orthodox rabbis, whose mandate was to ensure no religious laws would be violated.

Anat, who had become the spokeswoman for Jerusalem's Archeological Committee, resented having to go before "those self-serving hypocrites" to get permission for a dig. So, when she asked David to accompany her to one of her meetings with them, he readily agreed, thinking she wanted company to relieve the boredom of another dreary meeting.

David couldn't believe what he was seeing. The three rabbis sat on a raised platform at the head of a long room, like judges presiding in a trial. They reminded him of the Three Stooges. They were dumbfounded as Anat stood before them, making her case.

"It is a travesty that Jerusalem is known as the City of David. King David was an immoral *momzer* not worthy of having any city named after him, much less one as glorious as Jerusalem. I want you to issue a declaration that Jerusalem should be known as the City of Hezekiah."

She cited how the young and charismatic David had seduced King Saul's son, Jonathan, so he would step aside and allow him to become King. On the way, David also found time to seduce Jonathan's sister, Michal. When he was anointed king, David killed anyone who frustrated his sexual appetite. Anat reminded the rabbis how David had ensured the death of Uriah the Hittite, his most devoted warrior, so he could take Uriah's wife for himself, and how he had even handed over his own daughter, Tamar, to his favorite son, Amnon, a man as perverted as himself. "Amnon raped Tamar, then forced her onto the streets. And what did our beloved King David do? Nothing!"

"Madam, don't you think we have enough troubles? Why are you bothering us with what happened thousands of years ago?" said the rabbi who was picking his ears.

"Aren't your rulings based on what was written thousands of years ago?"

David watched as the eldest rabbi, infuriated, curled his beard.

"Madam, should we forget David's Book of Psalms?"

"Should we forget Hitler loved animals and children, and was vegetarian?" Anat asked, nonchalantly.

The rabbis shuddered at her casting King David in the same light as Hitler, but before they could reprimand her, Anat continued to press her argument.

"The Book of Psalms does not pardon him for committing evil," she said. "Of course, I understand you are the ultimate authorities on matters of morality. However, I am an authority in archaeology.

"David's Citadel and David's Tower have nothing to do with David. One was built in the sixteenth century; the other dates back to King Herod's time. King Hezekiah built the Broad Wall during the eighth century to defend Jerusalem from the Assyrians. So there is no archeological justification for calling Jerusalem the City of David.

"Why not honor Jerusalem with the name of a truly great king, one who lived up to his name, which meant strength and courage? When the time came, Hezekiah showed his mettle. Faced with certain defeat by the Assyrians, he encouraged the people of Jerusalem to make their own weapons and shields, and to build strong walls to repel the enemy.

"Thanks to Hezekiah, Jerusalem was able to resist the conquest. He ordered the construction of the Siloam Tunnel, chiseled out of seventeen hundred feet of solid rock to provide the city with underground access to the waters of the Gihon Spring. During his reign, Jerusalem became the most populated city of Judah. Hezekiak taught us to unite and defend ourselves from our enemies."

"Jerusalem," Anat demanded, "should be renamed the 'City

of Hezekiah,' which would be in keeping with the victory of its present unification."

"Madam, are you planning to petition having the Star of David changed to the Star of Hezekiah as well?" the rabbi chewing on his side locks asked.

"That will come later," Anat assured him.

The cold wind chilled them to the bone. Anat, who had not worn a hat, begged to stop at Café Cassis, where, at three in the afternoon, it was certain they would find Jonathan and Nilli. Ariel, she said, would not be joining them, as he was "abroad on business."

David's relationship with Jonathan had become strained since he shared his experience at the Armenian Church, for which he had not been able to find any rational explanation. In his subsequent meeting with Reb Eli, he had tried to learn more about Elijah and Jesus, but when he asked about them, Reb Eli had replied in the manner David had come to recognize as encouraging. "That's an inquiry best made on your own." David's loss of Tamar, coupled with the tragedies brought by the war, had driven him into a depression. He found relief by learning everything he could about Elijah and Jesus, two Jews with hopes of a messianic age of peace and love. The only people who seemed willing to take his interest seriously were Anat and Reb Eli.

Sitting in the café with Jonathan and Nilli, Anat's story of the rape of Tamar triggered David's imagination. He thought of her being as beautiful and sensuous as the Tamar he had known and was seeing himself rescuing her from Amnon, when Nilli interrupted his heroic fantasy by challenging Anat, "Why do you insist on creating a political ruckus about Bible stories?"

"If we don't face up to our past and identify those who kept their eyes closed to evil, we will repeat our history," Anat responded quickly, still impassioned by her presentation to the *Rabbanute.*

David thought Anat's point was well taken. "Why should Jerusalem be known for someone like that?"

"The *Rabbanute* feel it's enough just to read the Torah, I want them to abide by it," Anat said, firmly. "Otherwise, we will become just like the Christians who were taught to worship a loving Jesus and then committed murder against his tribe."

"Anat, you needn't worry that after two thousand years we will become like the Christians," Nilli said, growing tired of her rhetoric.

"We need to live up to who we are and what we want to become. Otherwise the world will define us once again," Anat said, soberly.

"Today, I'm having enough problems defining who I am and who I want to be," Jonathan said. He spoke of his desire to go the United States, where a more modern interpretation of Judaism was growing, but Nilli's life and work were in Jerusalem, so that option was out.

David revealed that for the past several months he had been studying Hebrew at the University and, to his surprise, had become somewhat fluent.

"Does that mean you're planning to stay on?" Jonathan asked.

"I'm not quite sure what my plans are."

"Still enjoying your visits with the rebbe?" Jonathan inquired.

"Yes, quite a lot," David said, not mentioning his ongoing desire to learn about Jesus, nor his determination to find Tamar.

"I'm glad you and the rebbe have become such good friends," Jonathan said warmly, hoping Reb Eli had helped David overcome his delusions.

Miriam took it upon herself to fulfill Sarah's role in serving their father his afternoon tea. She constantly tried to engage him in conversation about Sarah, often inquiring casually, "Any news from Sarah?"

The rebbe did his best to avoid speaking about her. He would simply answer, "She is fine."

Today again, Reb Eli made it clear by silently shaking his head in response to Miriam's inquiry that no more questions about Sarah would be welcomed or answered.

The gas heater in the rebbe's study was not strong enough to ward off the cold spell that had gripped Jerusalem. During David's visit, Reb Eli asked if he would help him move the table and chairs closer to the heater. David welcomed the rebbe's request, as well as the opportunity to sit closer to the heater in the chilly room. The two men sat bundled up in heavy sweaters, as close to the heater as possible.

David recounted Anat's argument at the Rabbanute and asked what the rebbe thought about the two kings, David and Hezekiah. Usually, when he asked the rebbe's opinion about anything, Reb Eli would direct him to learn, question and discover his own thoughts on the matter, just as he had every time David attempted to inquire about Elijah and Jesus. Today, perhaps, because of the greater intimacy of the rearranged study, the rebbe seemed more willing to express his personal views.

"Hezekiah," the rebbe said, "was a spiritual man who learned early on to turn to God for direction and strength. Therefore, the story of his inner life is not so intriguing. But David had so many personal demons and challenges to overcome; it's why we can relate to him. And like most of us at the end, when he is about to slip into eternity, he turns to God."

"So there is more we can learn from David's life, is that what you are saying?"

"For many of us, yes," the rebbe nodded, "but we each have our own work to do, and there's no escaping it."

David confided he had been reading the Aramaic translation of the New Testament, hoping to discover more about Jesus, but had been left uninspired and had begun doubting the significance of his encounter with the beggar at the church. Perhaps what Jonathan had said was true: he had been overwhelmed by the events of the war, and, exhausted as he was, his mind had triggered an imaginary vision.

"Even imaginary visions have significance, especially those that stay with us. It's important to go deeper into their meaning," the rebbe offered.

"Tamar wasn't a vision and she stays with me as well," David said, hoping for more guidance.

"Lust can disguise itself as a path to God."

"Being with her made me feel alive. It opened me to something I had never felt before. I felt one with everything," David said, trying his best to explain himself.

It had rained heavily all day and into the night. At nine in the evening, rain mixed with sleet was pelting the windows at Mickey's. Mickey's had become David's steady "dining room." He often ate there twice a day. The restaurant was usually packed during the day with hungry locals, but, in the evenings, there were few, if any, patrons.

"*Ma hadash,* Daveed?" It was now Mickey's standard greeting, "*Ma hadash,* what's new?" David was pleased he had graduated to being called by his Hebrew name, instead of "Mr. Churchill."

"*Hakol beseder,*" David said in the customary response, whether "everything" was "ok" or not.

The television on the counter blared the news. Mickey had installed it there after the war so he and his customers could keep up with the latest developments. It was a national addiction. After David sat down at his regular table, Mickey switched off the television and brought him his tea. "It's enough," he declared. "How many times can you hear the same thing?"

"How's Perez coming along?" David inquired, as he sipped his tea.

Mickey sat down, joining him with his Turkish coffee. "Thank God, every day a little better and stronger."

Mickey's eldest son, Perez, had been badly wounded during the fight for Jerusalem and was undergoing physical therapy at Hadassah Hospital. Nilli had been part of the team that had saved his leg. When Mickey had seen David at the emergency unit, disheveled and worn out, helping run supplies to the battlefield and bringing the wounded to the hospital, their relationship shifted into a deeper, more intimate connection.

The two men talked until midnight about politics, food,

women, and business. Mickey always saved David the best catch of *bouri,* seasoned the way he liked it, with extra lemon and parsley to tone down the garlic. His *borekas* were made slightly crisp and his pita bread and English tea were served piping hot.

Mickey's business had flourished after the war and he was thinking of expanding his little nook of a restaurant into something more substantial. There was no room for expansion in his present location. Mickey had checked out Ben Yehuda Street and other commercial areas of the city that offered larger spaces but the rents were much more than he could afford.

David listened attentively then asked, "Why not buy a building? You could pay off the mortgage and eventually be debt free with no rent to pay."

"Do I look like a millionaire?"

"I'll help you," David offered.

"You? How can you help me? Do you own a bank?"

"No, but I have access to the resources you need."

"Is this part of your English humor?"

"No, this sort of thing is not clever or funny enough to be considered English humor."

"What are you, the *meshiach?*" Mickey laughed, unable to grasp David's offer.

"I can loan you the money, interest free," David said, earnestly.

Mickey could not believe what he was hearing. "It could be years before I could pay you back. What will you get out of it?"

David shrugged, "A nice place to eat good food and enjoy good company ..."

Mickey looked at him, overwhelmed by his generosity. "So,"

he asked, "you've decided to stay?"

David nodded, "For the time being, yes."

Mickey's eyes gleamed with approval. He tapped his knuckles on the table emphatically, "Good."

The hood on David's rain jacket did not keep the rain and hail from hitting his face. He never used an umbrella, despite all the years of his mother's nagging. Alone on the streets, he walked briskly back to Abu Tor in good spirits, feeling a lightness of heart and a sense of well-being which even the strong winds did not disturb.

The winter was especially cold and damp. He kept his heater and hot water switched on all the time. Walking up the hill, he passed Anat's and Ariel's house and saw the light on in their window. He hadn't seen Anat for a few days and, knowing she never went to bed before two in the morning, especially when Ariel was out of town, he thought of stopping by, but the desire to rid himself of the chill in his body with a long hot soak in the tub took precedence.

Lying in the tub, he thought about what Anat had confided in him about her and Ariel's shared sexual fantasies. She had told Ariel of her bisexual encounters, and, to her delight, they had aroused him. She shared all the details with her husband during their love making, sometimes even creating fantasies to keep him excited, which served them both.

David closed his eyes, remembering Tamar, her smell, her touch, the way she looked at him, and the sensuousness of her body. He wondered how, in such a small, intimate city as Jerusalem, someone could just disappear. And as much as he tried to forget her, Tamar seeped into his mind at the oddest moments and his body longed for her.

When Anat had introduced him to several of her attractive friends, hoping he would forget Tamar, meeting them had only left him feeling worse, with an even deeper desire for her.

Wrapped in one of the white bath towels that were still stiff from the laundromat, he stood before the glass doors leading to the roof and watched a flurry of snow fall. Within seconds, Jerusalem of Gold became Jerusalem of White. He smelled the sweet, subtle scent he had experienced during his encounter at the Armenian Church and felt the same loving peace. The snow began to swirl, and there before him was the vision of a man. He waited in anticipation, hoping to receive a message, but the flurry stopped abruptly, and the presence disappeared with it.

At one in the morning, unable to sleep, and restless with desire to share his experience, he telephoned Anat asking if she would come up. She appeared with an offering of hashish. David needed to just talk and asked her not to smoke – he needed her to be fully present and hear him.

"Well, what do you think he came to tell you this time?" Anat asked, trying to be helpful.

"I haven't a clue and it's driving me mad."

"Did he look like the same person?"

"I'm not sure. I just know it had the same essence as him. It makes it all the more maddening," David said, trying to cope with his frustration.

Anat believed him. She just wondered if his visions had been hallucinations, as no snow had fallen in Jerusalem that night.

Reb Eli was concerned about David. How could he guide Phillip's son? He was as intelligent and dedicated as any of his Torah students but, clearly, he was destined to follow his own path.

When David entered his study that afternoon, the rebbe recognized a profound change had taken place. There was a serenity in him that he had seen only in those few who had been touched by grace. He listened as David told him about the previous night's encounter and how it had affected him. Then he went on to describe his own understanding about Elijah and Jesus, based on his reading. As David saw it, Jesus was a devout Jew who was troubled by the ways of the high priests at the Temple. He had his own following, and wanted to build his own Temple. Both Jesus and Elijah brought comfort and healing to those in need. Perhaps they were one and the same person?

"But what does any of this have to do with you?" asked Reb Eli.

The question stopped David in his tracks. He looked at the rebbe in amazement. "The beggar is me." David felt the entire universe come into the room.

Reb Eli smiled, "Welcome home."

TEN

After thirteen hours of labor, Sarah's son was born. Eleanor and Katie had stayed at the hospital throughout the night's ordeal. They had held Sarah's hand, reminding her to keep breathing through the pain and had wiped away the cold sweat from her face as she mumbled her prayers. The pain had been so intense that Sarah was afraid she would die and begged Eleanor to promise to look after her child. Eleanor promised, and kept reassuring her she would not die. Katie, who had given birth to three children, commiserated with Sarah, assuring her, "It's just the first one that's so painful, the others will just fall out."

After giving birth, Sarah collapsed into a deep sleep. Dr. Anne McKenzie placed her newborn son, Lior Ben-David, in Eleanor's arms. Lior's wide-open eyes stared inquisitively into hers, taking Eleanor aback, as most newborns' eyes could not yet focus, and they would ordinarily just cry.

Lior had entered the world with a seemingly knowing and commanding presence that Eleanor found a little intimidating. His head was covered with dark brown hair; a long strand fell over his right eye.

When Sarah awakened several hours later, Eleanor placed Lior in her arms. Sarah looked at her son and wept with joy and sorrow, mourning the loss of her mother, Yossi, and the love she had found and lost.

In that moment, Eleanor knew Sarah and Lior belonged to

her heart. She could do nothing less than look after them as her own.

A *mohel,* a rabbi, and a *minyan* of ten men were brought to Eleanor's home to perform Lior's *brit.* Phillip, unaware the infant was his grandson, held him as the *mohel* cut away his foreskin.

Katie had prepared a sumptuous *Kiddush* with apple, raspberry and huckleberry pies, and rich buttered scones topped with fresh cream. Kosher wine from Israel flowed into the cups of the *mohel,* the rabbi and the *minyan* of men. By the time the ten men, rabbi, and *mohel* boarded the chartered bus back to London, they were all happily tipsy.

Lior cried and was brought to his mother after the circumcision. Sarah held her son close to suckle her breast. She comforted him with lullabies and admired the perfection of his long torso and his tiny, elegant hands and feet. Her son was now a member of the tribe of Israel. Sarah was certain he would grow up to be as handsome and gentle as his father, and prayed he would have the wisdom and loving kindness of his grandfather, Reb Eliezer Ben-Jaacov.

She named her son Lior, after the Hebrew word "my light," and Ben-David, the son of David, just as her father had taken the Hebrew name Ben-Jaacov after his father, Jaacov.

During her labor, Sarah had feared she would die as punishment for her act of falseness and betrayal. She prayed for forgiveness and begged God, if he took her life, to spare her child. Sitting in the big armchair in her bedroom, breast-feeding her son, she thanked God for sparing them both and promised to protect her son with her life. She committed to teaching him to be a virtuous man of God.

Looking at her son, she was overcome with an intense love that gripped her entire being. She knew her life now belonged to him and no other. Memories of the war suddenly struck her heart. She thought of all the young men who had died or been wounded and could not fathom how mothers could give their children to war.

Sarah had left the safe cocoon of her orthodox world forever. If she returned home, Lior would be required to join the others and serve the country as a soldier. She realized, if the whole world declared war against Israel, she could never let her son go to war. It would be she who would go. She would be willing to die doing so to spare her son. To keep Lior safe, she had no choice but to remain and raise him in England. She would now have to find Jerusalem within herself.

Eleanor had immediately telephoned Eli with the news of Lior's birth. She could hear Eli try to hide the quiver in his voice as he asked how Sarah and the child were doing. He thanked Eleanor profusely, blessing her for having taken Sarah under her wing. It was he who had arranged for the *brit,* and for Phillip to be the child's *sandek.*

Today, she had to tell Eli that Sarah and his grandson would not be returning to Israel, where he had arranged for them to live in a Kibbutz in the upper Galilee. Sarah had decided to find a small flat in a Jewish section of London where she could tutor young students in Hebrew, preparing them for their bat mitzvahs. She would wait until Lior was old enough to attend school before returning to full-time teaching at a yeshiva.

Eleanor sensed how heartbreaking the news was for Eli. She tried to comfort him by saying he was always welcome to come to England to see Sarah and his grandson, and perhaps, in time, Sarah would return to Israel. She assured him she would look after Sarah and Lior as if they were her own and promised to call frequently to let him know how they were doing.

Why not wait until the baby is a little older, and then move to London?" Eleanor urged. "After all, the students won't be returning to school until September." What Eleanor didn't say was how much she dreaded Sarah's leaving. She had grown to cherish the girl and her child. Sarah had brought such joy to her home, and Eleanor did not want to let go of that gift.

Sarah could not refuse Eleanor anything she requested. She was so grateful and felt indebted to her for all she had done on her behalf. Besides, the offer made perfect sense. She had grown to love the beauty of the countryside and the comforts of Eleanor's home. Lior would enjoy his first summer riding along the country roads in his pram, and, more importantly, Sarah had found a surrogate mother in Eleanor. With all the love and graciousness Eleanor had shown her, she was feeling profound guilt that she had not revealed the truth about the father of her child. She could not continue living a lie, and decided it was time to confess everything to Eleanor, whom she trusted implicitly.

Mickey's had moved to the heart of town, occupying a large space which had been a former bakery. It now served wine and liquor to complement its Mideastern cuisine. Since the war, tourists arrived in droves, taking pride in Israel's victory as if it were their own. Mickey had bagels flown in from New York for the American tourists, who disliked pita bread and thought bagels were "more Jewish."

David had encouraged Mickey to stage an invitation-only opening night to introduce his new place to Jerusalemites, who, he was confident, would appreciate the good food and stylish decor. For the occasion, extra chairs and tables were brought in. Each table had a white linen tablecloth and napkins and a tall, slender vase holding a single long-stemmed red rose. Brass oil lanterns purchased at an Arab shop in the Old City added warmth and charm.

The room was quickly packed to capacity with people standing shoulder-to-shoulder, eating and drinking. In Israel, David learned, "Invitation Only" meant anyone who was invited could invite anyone else as well. Jo Amar, a Moroccan-born *chazan,* accompanied by his musicians, sang songs in Hebrew, Arabic, French and Ladino. The music got everyone up and dancing, clapping with the rhythm.

Mickey had often spoken about his wife, Sultana, referring to her as a "hot woman." When he introduced her at the opening, David tried to hide his astonishment, as Sultana possessed hips that resembled a baby elephant. Sultana, like Mickey, was of Syrian descent with large, dark brown eyes and hair that framed her exotic, warm and pleasing face. Within minutes, David forgot her over-sized body and took a strong liking to her. Sultana's embrace felt maternally comforting. She scolded Mickey for not having brought David to their house, where she could have introduced him to her niece, Yasmine. She insisted David come to Shabbat and meet her. David thanked Sultana for the invitation, knowing he would never go.

Mickey's opening night was a great success. Everyone complimented his cooking and reveled in the hubbub. Mickey was so inspired he began talking to David about opening a "Mickey's" in Tel Aviv and one in Haifa, and offered him a partnership. "Everybody comes to eat, drink, and tell lies to forget their troubles. What could be better?"

Mickey's offer was genuine. David put his arm around him. "We'll talk about it."

Anat's petition to rename Jerusalem as the "City of Hezekiah" had been rejected, and the appetite she had lost during the war had returned. David watched with amazement as she devoured her third crème brûlée. "No one knows how to make crème brûlée like Mickey," she said, savoring every mouthful.

David was laughing, when, from the corner of his eye, he spotted a familiar face coming through the door. With a rush of panic, he nervously whispered to Anat, "Madame Aziza."

Anat licked the last of the crème brûlée from her spoon, calmly assuring him he had nothing to worry about, "I'm sure there are many here who are acquainted with her. Her business would be destroyed if she were not discreet."

David saw Madame Aziza embrace Sultana, kissing her affectionately like old, close friends. When Sultana brought her over to David and introduced her as "my cousin, Jamila," he was completely baffled.

In her perfect enchantress manner, holding out her hand to him, she said, "Nice to meet you."

ELEVEN

At first, Eleanor was intrigued by Sarah's story of how, as a child, she had stolen away to follow her brother to Madame Aziza's house, and how enchanted she had been, watching beautiful women dance with long colorful scarves before men. It was only when Sarah became anxious and went on to confess that "Lior's father didn't die in the war," that Eleanor reached out her hand, to let her know it was safe to speak her truth.

"After Yossi died, I felt my life was over. I accepted my fate. Because I was unable to conceive, I was destined to live in loneliness. No young man would marry me. Then, out of nowhere, this outsider appeared. It began by simply noticing things like the way he brushed the hair off his forehead, the shyness of his smile. One day, I overheard him speaking with my father, I became so taken by the sound of his voice.

"Your father knew this man?"

"Yes. He was like many young men who came to seek guidance from him. But, he ... I just couldn't get him out of my mind. At first, I thought my attraction was because of my own desperation. I knew he could never be interested in someone like me, so, after some time, I decided the only way to get his attention was to change myself into a desirable woman."

Eleanor became enthralled, "What did you do?"

When I learned he was going to go to the house ..." Sarah looked at Eleanor, fearing what she might think once she learned of her exploits, "I went to Madame Aziza, and asked her to teach me all about men. I convinced her to employ me."

"Employ you?"

"As a prostitute. I told her she could keep all the money as long as the Englishman would be my only client, and that he never be told."

Eleanor, trying to hide her disbelief, asked casually, "What was this Englishman's name?"

"David."

Eleanor was dumbfounded. Sarah, she realized, was the "prostitute" David had fallen in love with! And her son, Lior Ben-David, was indeed David's son.

Eleanor had been so taken by Sarah's confession, she could not speak. What astonished her most was how she felt nothing but admiration and awe for Sarah's audacity. Sarah, the daughter of Eli, the Chief Rabbi of Jerusalem, had portrayed herself as a prostitute so she could be with the man she desired and loved. Fearing that Sarah would be humiliated if she told her that the David she loved was her nephew, Eleanor was speechless. How could she have not recognized David's son? Lior looked just like David! How blind we can be to what is before us.

"Sarah, I know how difficult this was for you. I want you to know how courageous I think you are."

Relieved by her confession, Sarah wept. "I had hoped he would love me as I loved him."

Sarah told her how many times she had inadvertently opened the Bible to the story of Tamar. "I believed I was cursed with misfortune, so I became Tamar, and stole what I wanted from life."

"I couldn't contain my passion for the Englishman and feared dying never to have known him. When I refused to die empty-handed, God blessed me with a love I had never known and gave me more than I asked for, my son."

Later that night, lying in bed, unable to sleep, Eleanor realized there was something much deeper lurking inside her. Sarah had done what Eleanor wished she had done long ago in her youth, summoned the courage and imagination to pursue the man she desired.

At seven o'clock, just after the morning prayers, the phone rang in Reb Eli's study. It was Eleanor calling from England with news of great importance to him.

Reb Eli listened carefully, at times asking Eleanor to repeat what she had said to make sure that what he was hearing was a reality, not just voices in his head. Sarah's confession to Eleanor astounded him. He thought perhaps his daughter had become delusional. It was only when he heard the quiet, comforting tone with which Eleanor spoke that he knew it was all true. Sarah had fallen in love with David and was so desperate to be seen by him as an attractive, desirable woman, she had impersonated a prostitute. The rebbe was so flabbergasted he could not find any words to respond. He asked if they could speak later as he needed time to get over the shock of this astonishing news.

The rebbe hung up the phone and sat quietly, his body frozen to his chair. He could not even feel the tears streaming down his cheeks. How, he wondered, could he have been so blind to his own daughter's plight?

Only now did he remember that Sarah had never cried when she lost her mother or her husband, or when people gossiped about her barrenness and lack of *mazel.* She had never uttered a word. Instead, she had held it all inside until she no longer could. Sarah had taken her anguish to what she knew and loved best, the mysteries and parables of the Bible, and had chosen to follow in the footsteps of Tamar. All this time, the rebbe had thought of David as a troubled young man with hallucinations about Jesus who had foolishly become smitten by one of Madame Aziza's girls.

He, the renowned Chief Rabbi of Jerusalem, with all his knowledge, could not see what was before him. He realized how little he knew of the human heart. The rebbe sat as an empty vessel, with an open, aching heart waiting, as he had many times before, waiting for *Hashem* to lead him on paths unknown. He sat until the lightening rod of *Hashem* struck, awakening him to himself.

Reb Eli's tears turned to laughter when he awoke to a joy that filled every cell of his being. God, in his masterful plan, had brought two of his lost children together, choosing Madame Aziza as his agent. The rebbe said a *bracha* for Madame Aziza, blessing her with all the miracles of God's grace.

Unable to contain the joy that filled him, he ran out of the house and looked up to the heavens. *"You who are master of the universe have brought me to my knees and opened my heart!"* he cried out. Then, he danced in the streets of Mea Shearim, where the Hasidim saw him and begged to know what had happened. The rebbe simply said, "*Hashem* has opened my heart to see!"

The Hasidim saw the light in the rebbe's eyes and they, too, began dancing. Soon, a large circle of black-coated men, with their arms wrapped around each other's shoulders, joined in the dancing, sharing the joy of the rebbe's revelation, as women and children looked on.

Miriam called out to her sisters, Esther and Devorah, "Come quick, something has happened. Father is dancing like today is Simchas Torah!"

Sitting with Anat at Café Cassis, discussing whether to stay on in Jerusalem, David overheard two middle-aged men wearing *kippahs* talking about Reb Eli dancing in the streets of Mea Shearim. He was puzzled, but not as much as when Jonathan arrived informing him the rebbe had called, asking that David come see him.

"Is he all right?"

Jonathan reported that "actually, he sounded quite chipper."

Eleanor knew the only thing to do was to tell Eli the truth about Sarah and David and seek his help. She had telephoned him, telling him in the most delicate way everything she knew, and how Sarah hadn't a clue who her beloved David was. For Sarah, he was just another Englishman who had come to seek advice from her father.

Over the next few days, Eleanor telephoned Eli, informing him that Sarah had decided to accept the teaching job Phillip had arranged at an orthodox, all-girls school in London, starting in autumn. She also confided that, from what she had learned from Phillip, David had no intention of returning home any time soon, and she suspected he was remaining in Jerusalem hoping to find "Tamar." She needed his help to bring Sarah and David together. She hoped he could come up with a way to get David to return to England, without revealing Sarah's secret to him, or anyone else. She, herself, would gladly keep Sarah's confidence, yet she confessed, she relished the moment Victoria would discover her grandson was also the grandson of the Chief Rabbi of Jerusalem.

There was a change in Reb Eli, which David couldn't quite figure out. There was something in his eyes that had not been there before. An intimacy and a lightness of spirit had replaced the piercing intensity of his gaze.

"Was your offer to help with my family matter sincere?"

David quickly asserted, "Yes, of course."

"Good," the rebbe said light-heartedly. "I have a special request. My youngest daughter, Sarah, has fallen for an unmarried man and given birth to his son. Given the religious society we live in, she had to leave for England. If you would be willing to go there and marry her, by Jewish law only, I will commit to helping you find Tamar. After you bring them home, whenever you request a *get*, I will give it to you."

"What is a *get*?" David asked, completely baffled.

"A divorce according to Jewish law."

"How can you find Tamar?" David asked, incredulously.

"I was the one who arranged your meeting with Madame Aziza and I will arrange the meeting with Tamar."

David could not speak. He thought perhaps he had imagined all that was being said.

"Take your time to think about my offer," the rebbe said, plainly.

"Where does your daughter live?" David heard himself ask.

"Safely, with your aunt Eleanor."

It had been well over a year since David had arrived in Jerusalem. Now, he was returning to England more confused than when he had left.

He told Mickey he was going home to take care of a family matter and would return soon. David told the same to Anat, as he had promised the rebbe his mission would be kept in confidence. He did not divulge anything to Jonathan, other than that he had decided to return home for a visit.

Reb Eli's request that he marry his daughter in exchange for his promise to find Tamar had left David utterly mystified. If the rebbe knew Tamar's whereabouts, why hadn't he offered to help him find her before? And why hadn't he asked one of his own Hasids to marry his daughter? Why him? None of it made sense. All David knew was that he trusted the rebbe and believed he would never make a promise he could not keep.

As soon as Eleanor learned that David was coming to England, she arranged a trip to London where she insisted on buying Sarah a wardrobe for her new life in the city. For special occasions, they bought an elegant pale cream cashmere dress which enhanced Sarah's natural beauty. Sarah had felt the dress was too revealing for the orthodox community where she would be living and working, but Eleanor overcame her inhibitions, "The dress has long sleeves and shows little skin.

Besides," Eleanor told her, "when you move to London you will need something special for all those Jewish holidays."

During their shopping spree, Eleanor seemed happier and more excited than Sarah had ever seen her. She wondered if, perhaps, having her and now Lior living in her home had become too much for her, and whether she was looking forward to getting back to the peace and quiet she had enjoyed before they arrived. She could understand how that would be best for Eleanor, yet she could not help feeling sad, realizing how lonely she would be, and how much she would miss her.

Phillip suspected something amiss when David told him he had come home to help Reb Eli by agreeing to marry his daughter, "so she can return home without disgrace." What David didn't tell his father was how anxious he was to complete this mission so he could quickly return to Jerusalem and his true love, Tamar.

Phillip knew Eli well enough to be certain he would never ask such a thing of anyone if there were not a critical, spiritual and ethical matter at stake. He listened carefully to David and only intervened when a hysterical Victoria burst out, "Marrying his daughter as a matter of convenience is preposterous. How could a respectable man ask such a thing? This could easily ruin your reputation, and ours."

David explained that it was only a marriage under Jewish law and would not be documented and, therefore, the marriage would not be recognized or even known about in England.

The details of the arranged marriage did not assuage Victoria's fears. "Why couldn't he have arranged for one of his own kind to marry his daughter? Why you for heaven's sake?" she demanded.

"Because he can trust me," David answered. "It is only a religious marriage of convenience and no one will ever know." The marriage, David told her, would take place as soon as he returned to Israel with the rebbe's daughter and grandson, as promised.

"These things always have a way of getting out," Victoria pleaded.

"The ceremony will be conducted by an orthodox rabbi, a friend of the rebbe. Surely we can trust him to keep it confidential." David argued.

"In such matters, I trust no one," Victoria exclaimed.

"That may be true for you. It's not for me."

"How dare you! It is because of our standing that you have enjoyed such a privileged life. Now you want to put everything in jeopardy? And for what?"

"Stop. This is not helping," Phillip insisted.

"I didn't mean to be offensive, I ... "

"Have you ever met Eli's daughter?"

"Frankly, I don't recall meeting her. Jonathan and I once attended a Shabbat dinner at the rebbe's house where all the women were seated at another table. I didn't pay much attention to any of them."

In truth, Phillip was not happy with the arrangement either, but he would not admit it. Something gnawed at him. Eli would never create a sham marriage, or anything like it. If he called Eli to inquire why he had chosen David to marry Sarah, it might embarrass and humiliate him further. In the thirty years of their friendship, Eli had never asked for anything, except refuge for his daughter. Perhaps Eli's request was just a religious matter after all, nothing more than a way to save face and preserve the standing of the Chief Rabbi of Jerusalem.

Eli's assignment gave Eleanor a vigor she hadn't felt for years. She was to arrange for Sarah and David to meet alone, as if by chance. She could feel her heart pounding with excitement and the blood rushing through her veins. This was her opportunity to act boldly and create a memorable encounter for Sarah and David. Their meeting had to be perfectly orchestrated.

Because David knew Sarah was living with her, Eleanor arranged for him to come for dinner to meet her. She told Sarah that her nephew, whom she cherished, had returned from abroad and she wanted to prepare a special evening for him. Eleanor asked Sarah if she would be kind enough to participate in the occasion, knowing she would do anything to please her. Eleanor was grateful Phillip had rarely come by to see Sarah and had never spoken to her about his son, David.

It had been a bitterly cold March, and there were no wildflowers to be found. Flower arrangements from the greenhouse filled the conservatory, where Eleanor had decided their meeting should take place. It was Sarah's favorite room in the house.

"We'll have the hors d'oeuvres served out here," she told Sarah.

Given the cold, bleak weather, Sarah wondered if the room, though beautiful, would be warm enough in the evening.

Eleanor assured her, "We'll light the fire. It will be quite toasty. This evening," she added, "would be the perfect time to wear that lovely cashmere dress to help keep you warm."

When Sarah tried to put Lior to sleep, he became cranky and cried. She rocked him in her arms and sang lullabies to comfort him when an odd sensation took hold of her. She suddenly had an uneasy feeling in her stomach and was overcome with fear. She was not comfortable meeting Eleanor's nephew. Given her experience with Phillip and Victoria, she worried that their son would be no different. She had felt very relieved after telling Eleanor the truth of what she had done, and was grateful Eleanor had responded with kindness and acceptance. She could not imagine her own mother, if she had been alive, would have been as understanding. She felt such gratitude and love for all that Eleanor was and had done for her and Lior. There was nothing she wouldn't do in return.

Eleanor had to be meticulous with the timing of David's arrival and Sarah's entrance. Her plan was for Sarah to come into the conservatory, where David would be waiting on his own. She arranged for him to come at seven o'clock, when she knew Sarah would be putting Lior to sleep. She would entertain him until Sarah arrived, which she asked her to do at eight, prior to dinner.

She welcomed David home with a fervor he had not seen or felt from her before. His aunt looked better than he remembered. She appeared to be in high spirits, something that was rare since her husband had died. They sat in the salon, sharing a glass of sherry.

Eleanor inquired how Jonathan and Nilli were doing. He told

her they were fine and how fond he was of Nilli. She asked how Nilli and her family were coping with the loss of her brother in the war. David described how much Gideon had meant to him and what a tragic loss it was for Nilli and her family, who were Holocaust survivors. "Frankly, I don't know how families cope with such things. It's all terribly heartrending."

"Perhaps now there's a chance for peace," Eleanor offered.

"Unfortunately, I'm the only one I know who believes so," David said.

"Let's hope and pray for a future that makes peace a reality. I'm so looking forward to coming in May for a visit. It's been so long since I've been to Jerusalem."

David purposely avoided discussing the details of his arranged marriage and inquired how it had been for his aunt, looking after the rebbe's daughter and her child. Eleanor simply said it was fine. Sarah, she said, was putting her baby to sleep and would be joining them soon for hors d'oeuvres in the conservatory.

"David, do you remember when we last spoke, I told you, with time, you would find that same passion again?"

"Yes ..."

"Time has never brought back the passion I had found."

David looked at her, bewildered.

"He was the young man who lived with us during the war. I kept it secret from him and my family."

"Wasn't that ..."

"Yes, Reb Eli."

"Why did you keep it a secret?"

"Fear, that he didn't and couldn't love me. Fear that our

worlds were too far apart."

"Why haven't you ever told me about this?"

"I just did. Now, if you wouldn't mind waiting for me in the conservatory, I'll go and see how things are coming along in the kitchen."

Sarah's singing had finally soothed Lior to sleep. She looked at her son, remembering the night he was conceived on a rooftop overlooking Jerusalem. How much love she felt for his father. She tenderly kissed him, wishing him sweet dreams, until she returned later that night.

In the conservatory, David thought he had heard the distant sound of a baby's cry, followed by the beautiful melodious voice of a woman singing. The fireplace was lit brilliantly; candles burned among the plants and flowers. David had never seen it look so vibrantly alive and beautiful. There was a familiar scent floating in the air, which did not come from the flowers. It made David feel strangely nostalgic. He thought of his aunt's revelation, of Tamar, and how soon the rebbe's promise to him would be fulfilled.

David stared out into the night and saw snowflakes falling. For a split second, he imagined that, in the distance, he could see Jerusalem.

He heard soft footsteps approaching. Expecting his aunt Eleanor, he turned around. Standing before him, in an elegant cream, dress was Tamar. His mind spun, *"She asked for you. You were her only client."*

Sarah could not breathe. David was Eleanor's nephew? Why hadn't her father told her? There was so much her father hadn't said, so much she didn't know or understand.

She and David stood looking at each other, trying to grasp what was before them.

Sarah knew now that her life had been created and unfolded by the grace of the *Ein Sof,* belonging only to the Infinite.

The pieces fell together for David. He now knew the story of Tamar. He recognized the woman he loved, and he spoke her name.

"Sarah."

AUTHOR'S NOTE

I lived in Israel in the 1960s, a naive twenty-year-old, hoping to find myself and the place in the world where I belonged. To me, the possibility of war was remote. I imagined the tensions in the region would somehow be resolved peacefully. Then, the Six Day War erupted. I experienced it firsthand in Jerusalem, where the moods and atmosphere of the city took on a new dimension.

I have drawn *Night in Jerusalem* from my experiences during that time. The historical events portrayed in the novel are accurate. Although shaped by my imagination, its characters are based on the people I knew in the city. Like me, they were struggling to make sense of their lives, responding to inherited challenges they could not escape that shaped their destiny in ways they and the entire Middle East could not have imagined.

CPSIA information can be obtained
at www.ICGtesting.com
Printed in the USA
BVOW08*0512070317
477571BV00002B/2/P

9 780996 559218